The King's Bride

The King's Bride

A Fairy Tale Based on Real Life

E.T.A. Hoffmann

Translated by Paul Turner

ALMA CLASSICS

ALMA CLASSICS
an imprint of

ALMA BOOKS LTD
Thornton House
Thornton Road
Wimbledon Village
London SW19 4NG
United Kingdom
www.101pages.co.uk

The King's Bride first published in German in 1821
First published by John Calder (Publishers) Limited in 1959
Translation © John Calder (Publishers) Limited, 1959
First published by Alma Classics in 2009. Reprinted February 2010
A new edition first published by Alma Classics in 2015
This new edition first published by Alma Classics in 2024

Cover: David Wardle

Printed in Great Britain by CPI Group (UK) Ltd, Croydon CR0 4YY

MIX
Paper | Supporting
responsible forestry
FSC® C013604

ISBN: 978-1-84749-925-7

All rights reserved. No part of this publication may be reproduced, stored in or introduced into a retrieval system, or transmitted, in any form or by any means (electronic, mechanical, photocopying, recording or otherwise), without the prior written permission of the publisher. This book is sold subject to the condition that it shall not be resold, lent, hired out or otherwise circulated without the express prior consent of the publisher.

Contents

Introduction 7

The King's Bride 11

Notes 99

Introduction

The first thing one notices about E.T.A. Hoffmann is his versatility. In the course of a relatively short life (1776–1822), he successfully practised four different professions: those of lawyer, artist, musician and writer – and it may be as well to trace his career in each of these fields separately.

Following the example of his uncle Otto, who brought him up from the age of three, he studied law at university, and practised as a lawyer from 1795 until 1806, when Warsaw, where he was then employed on the Prussian administrative staff, was occupied by the French and all Prussian officials lost their jobs. In 1814 he resumed his legal career in Berlin, and in 1816 received the important appointment of chairman of the Supreme Court of Justice, which he held until his death. Although he often grudged the time that his legal work took away from more creative activities, he was evidently very good at it.

His career as an artist began in 1795, when he sent two historical paintings to a friend's wealthy uncle, in the hope that he would buy them. The uncle thought they were intended as a gift, and gratefully added them to his collection. At Posen, in 1802, Hoffmann got into trouble with the authorities for circulating subversive caricatures of the local military commandant, and as a punishment was transferred to the remote town of Płock, where he spent his spare time copying pictures of ancient vases and painting portraits. At Warsaw he painted murals in the Academy of Music, and at Bamberg, in 1808, he designed sets for several theatrical productions. Finally, in 1814, he celebrated the Battle of Leipzig by publishing a series of cartoons on the downfall of the Napoleonic regime.

One indication of his devotion to music is the fact that he changed his third Christian name from Wilhelm to Amadeus, as a tribute to Mozart. When he left university, he started giving music lessons – with the result that he fell in love with one of his pupils – and composing songs and incidental music for plays. In 1799 he wrote his first opera, *Die Maske* ("The Mask"), and between then and 1816, when his last opera, *Undine*, was successfully performed in Berlin, he composed two symphonies and a great variety of vocal and instrumental music. In 1808 he was appointed Director of Music at the theatre at Bamberg, and in 1813 he joined the Seconda Opera Company at Dresden in the same capacity. He was also a distinguished music critic, and from 1809 onwards was a regular contributor to the *Allgemeine musikalische Zeitung*.

His writings, however, are his chief claim to fame. His first published work (1803) was an essay on the use of the classical chorus in drama. Then he wrote one or two plays, and a few dramatic fragments, but he found his true *métier* when he started writing fiction. *Fantasiestücke* ("Fantasy Pieces"), a collection of essays and stories published in 1814–15, included the well-known *Der goldene Topf* ("The Golden Pot"), translated into English by Carlyle in 1827. In 1816 he brought out *Die Elixiere des Teufels* ("The Devil's Elixir"), a horrific novel of the supernatural partly inspired by Matthew Gregory Lewis's *The Monk*. It was followed by *Nachtstücke* ("Night Pieces", 1817), a collection of stories in a similar vein, and finally by *Die Serapionsbrüder* ("The Serapion Brethren", 1819–21). The stories in this collection are inserted into a framework of conversation between various members of a club, some of whom represent aspects of Hoffmann's own character, and others actual friends of his. Vinzenz, for instance, who tells the story of 'The King's Bride' is a certain Dr Koreff, Professor of Medicine at Berlin University, whose special interest was "animal magnetism" or hypnotism – hence the allusion on p. 39.

Hoffmann was extremely sociable by nature, and his taste for alcoholic conviviality has been blamed for his early death. His love life may be said to have begun during his school days, when he and a friend tried to dig a tunnel underneath the wall of a neighbouring girls' school under the pretext of planting an exotic shrub. At the age of twenty he was forced to leave Königsberg for Glogau, as a result of the scandal caused by his association with a married woman. At twenty-six he married Michalina Rohrer, a pretty, good-natured but not very intellectual young lady, whose dim reflection may perhaps be seen in the portrait of Fräulein Ann in 'The King's Bride'. The marriage was on the whole a happy one, but Hoffmann never became very domesticated, and at thirty-five he fell desperately in love with another pupil of his, a fifteen-year-old singer called Julia Marc, who was shortly afterwards persuaded by her family to marry a rich merchant from Hamburg.

In person, Hoffmann was extremely short, with a rather ugly face and a prominent nose. He always had a sense of physical inferiority, and there may perhaps be an element of personal resentment in the remarks on p. 70 about the average female's attitude to males. Indeed, the whole description of Corduanspitz, the little gnome who "bore no resemblance whatever to the *Apollo Belvedere*", may possibly be regarded as an ironic self-portrait. At any rate, this half-comic, half-sinister figure is a very apt embodiment of Hoffmann's literary personality, his characteristic blend of fantasy and realism, pathos and impish satire, buffoonery and magic.

– Paul Turner

The King's Bride

I

*In which various characters are introduced and
their circumstances described, and the stage is
pleasantly set for all the extraordinary scenes that
will be enacted in the following chapters.*

It was a wonderful year. Magnificent crops of wheat, barley and oats were ripening in the fields; the peasant boys were busy picking peas, and the cows were equally busy nibbling clover. There were so many cherries on the trees that, much as the sparrows would have liked to peck them all off at one go, they were forced to leave half of them over for another meal. Nature kept open house, and every day her guests had all the food that they could possibly eat. But her real triumph was Herr Dapsul von Zabelthau's kitchen garden, where the beauty of the vegetables was so unprecedented that Fräulein Ann was quite understandably in ecstasies about it.

I suppose I had better explain right away who these two people were. Just imagine, dear reader, that you are travelling through the lovely country beside the river Main. Warm breezes are wafting fragrance over the meadows, which glisten in the golden light of the rising sun. You cannot bear to stay cooped up in your carriage, so you get out and start wandering through a wood, beyond which, as you come down into the valley, you catch sight of a small village.

Suddenly you see a tall, thin man approaching, whose extraordinary costume immediately rivets your attention. Perched on top of a jet-black wig he wears a small grey felt hat, and everything else about him – coat, waistcoat, trousers, socks and shoes – is grey to match. Even his preternaturally long walking stick is painted grey. He comes striding towards you, with his great deep-set eyes staring straight at you, but appears to be quite unaware of your existence.

"Good morning, sir!" you call out, just in time to prevent a collision. At this he gives a start, as if he had suddenly woken out of a deep dream, raises his hat and addresses you in hollow, tragic tones.

"Good morning?" he repeats. "My dear sir, how thankful we should be that it is a good morning! Those poor people at Santa Cruz – just had two earthquakes, and now it's pouring with rain!"

You do not quite know how to reply to this odd remark, and while you are still thinking it over, he says "Allow me, sir" and gently touches your forehead, and then takes a look at your palm.

"God bless you, sir," he continues, in the same hollow, tragic tone as before. "You have a good horoscope."

And with that he goes striding off again.

Now, this unusual man is none other than Herr Dapsul von Zabelthau, and the only bit of property that he possesses

CHAPTER I

is the tiny village of Dapsulheim, which lies in the most delightful surroundings immediately ahead of you. In fact, you are just coming into it.

You want some breakfast, but things do not look too promising at the local inn, for they have just had a village fair, and stocks are consequently very low. As you insist on having something more substantial than a glass of milk, they direct you to the manor house, where Fräulein Anna, they say, will be only too glad to give you whatever she has available.

So off you go to the manor house, of which all I need to say for the moment is that, like the chateau of M. le Baron de Thunder-ten-Tronck* in Westphalia, it possesses windows and doors, and that over the front door are displayed the arms of the von Zabelthau family, carved, Maori-fashion, in wood. But the odd thing about this house is that its north side abuts on the outer wall of an old ruined castle, so that the back door is actually the original castle gate and leads straight into the castle courtyard, in the middle of which a tall, round watchtower still remains intact.

At the front door, the one with the coat of arms above it, you are met by a rosy-cheeked young lady, who with her fair hair and bright-blue eyes would really be quite pretty, if only her figure were a shade less round and solid. Her manner is kindness itself. She asks you in and, as soon as she hears what you want, produces some delicious milk, a large slice of bread and butter, some ham which tastes good enough to have come from Bayonne and a small glass of beetroot brandy. Meanwhile your hostess, who is none other than Fräulein Anna von Zabelthau, chats cheerfully away about all sorts of things connected with agriculture, a subject on which she is evidently well informed.

Suddenly a loud and dreadful cry rings out:

"Anna! Anna! Anna!"

It appears to be a voice from heaven, and you are naturally terrified, but Fräulein Anna kindly explains:

"Papa's just got back from his walk and wants his breakfast. He's calling from his study."

"Calling from his study?" you repeat in astonishment.

"That's right," says Fräulein Anna, or Fräulein Ann, as most people call her. "You see, Papa's study is up there in the tower, and he's speaking through a megaphone."

And then, dear reader, you see her open a small door in the tower and run upstairs with the same sort of breakfast as you have just eaten yourself – that is to say, a large helping of ham and bread, and a glass of beetroot brandy. The next moment she is back again, taking you round her beautiful kitchen garden and talking away so fast about variegated featherheads, rapunticas, English turnips, little greenheads, montrues, great moguls, yellow kingheads and so on that you begin to feel quite bewildered, especially if you are not aware that these are merely grand names for cabbages and lettuces.

CHAPTER I

Well, dear reader, the brief visit that you have just paid to Dapsulheim should be enough, I think, to give you a general picture of the house which is the scene of the strange and almost incredible story that I am now about to relate.

In his youth Herr Dapsul von Zabelthau seldom set foot outside the house of his parents, who were fairly wealthy people. His tutor, who was an elderly eccentric, not only instructed him in foreign languages, especially those of the East, but also encouraged his natural bent for mysticism, or rather for mystery-mongering. The tutor died and left young Dapsul a whole library of books on the occult, in which he became deeply engrossed. His parents also died, and now young Dapsul set out on his travels, which in accordance with his tutor's recommendation included visits to Egypt and to India. When he finally came back, many years later, he found that a cousin had administered his estate in his absence with such zeal that there was nothing left but the tiny village of Dapsulheim.

Herr Dapsul von Zabelthau was far too interested in the sun-begotten gold of a higher sphere to care about losing the earthly variety. On the contrary, he thanked his cousin heartily for saving out of the wreck such a pleasant place as Dapsulheim, with its fine, high watchtower, which might have been expressly designed for taking astrological observations. And he promptly arranged for the top floor of it to be furnished as his study.

His thoughtful cousin now proved to him conclusively that it was his duty to get married. Dapsul admitted the necessity of this step, and immediately married the young lady that his cousin had selected for the purpose. His wife had scarcely entered the house before she left it again, for she died in giving birth to a daughter. The cousin saw to all the arrangements for the wedding, the baptism and the funeral, so that Dapsul in his tower hardly noticed what was going on, especially as these events coincided with the appearance of a most remarkable comet, with which he believed his own destiny to be connected, for he was always on the lookout for possible omens of disaster.

His daughter was brought up by an aged great-aunt, who was delighted to find that the child soon showed signs of interest in estate management. So Fräulein Ann was made to start at the bottom and work her way up, from goose girl to kitchen maid, to housemaid, to housekeeper, right up to the status of gentlewoman farmer. Thus theoretical knowledge was illustrated and confirmed by salutary practical experience. She developed an extraordinary passion for geese and ducks and hens and pigeons, for sheep and for cows – nor was she by any means indifferent to the joys of cherishing a plump young porker, although she never went quite so far as that girl in some country or other who tied a ribbon with a bell on it round the neck of a little white piglet and treated it like a lapdog.

But what meant more to her than anything else in the world, even than her orchard, was her kitchen garden. As the gentle reader will have noticed in his conversation with her, Fräulein

CHAPTER I

Ann had received from her great-aunt, who was a mine of information on all agricultural matters, a good grounding in the science of growing vegetables, and not only was she in sole charge of all such things as preparing the soil, sowing the seeds and planting the plants, but she also took an active part in these operations herself. Even her worst enemy was forced to admit that Fräulein Ann wielded a very pretty spade.

Thus, while Herr Dapsul von Zabelthau devoted himself entirely to astrological observations and other mystic rites, Fräulein Ann, on the death of her great-aunt, made an excellent job of running the estate. In other words, whereas Dapsul's head was always in the clouds, Ann's interests were extremely down to earth.

So no wonder Fräulein Ann was in ecstasies when she found that her kitchen garden was doing so extraordinarily well this year. But surpassing all the other vegetables in luxuriance of growth were the carrots, which promised a quite unprecedented yield.

"Oh, my pretty little darlings!" cried Fräulein Ann again and again, clapping her hands and jumping up and down, and generally behaving like a child that has been given a wonderful Christmas present. And apparently the young carrots were feeling equally cheerful, for the faint sound of laughter that was heard at that moment undoubtedly came from underneath the soil. Ann took no notice of it, but dashed off to meet a farmhand, who was waving a letter in the air and shouting:

"For you, Fräulein Ann! Gottlieb's just brought it from the town."

Ann recognized the writing and knew at once that the letter came from young Herr Amandus von Nebelstern, a neighbouring landowner's son, who was up at the university. Now, while he was still living at home and running over to Dapsulheim every day, Amandus had convinced himself that he could never in his whole life love anyone but Fräulein Ann. In the same way, Fräulein Ann knew for a certainty that it would be quite impossible for her to feel the slightest partiality for anyone but the brown-haired Amandus. They had therefore agreed that the sooner they got married and became the happiest couple in the whole wide world the better.

Amandus had been a cheerful, unaffected lad before he went up to the university, but there he came under the influence of someone or other who not only persuaded him that he was a tremendous poetical genius, but also induced him to cultivate an extremely bombastic style. His efforts in this direction were so successful that he had soon risen far above what was called reason and common sense by mere prose writers, who were so foolish as to suggest that these qualities are perfectly compatible with the greatest imaginative activity.

Such was the young man who had written this letter. Joyfully, Ann opened it and read as follows:

CHAPTER I

HEAVENLY MAIDEN,

Can you picture – can you feel – can you sense what your Amandus is doing at this moment? Can you see him, in the very flower of his youth, with the orange-blossom scents of fragrant Evening eddying round him, lying on his back in the grass and gazing skywards with eyes full of yearning devotion and of holy love? Lavender and thyme, roses and carnations, shy violets and yellow-eyed narcissi, all these he is weaving into a flowery crown. And every flower is a love thought – a thought of you, my Anna!

But is it fit that lips inspired by love should speak in barren prose? Hearken, oh, hearken! For I can only love in sonnet form, and only in a sonnet tell my love!

> Bright as a thousand suns see Love arise!
> See lips of passion press to passion's lips!
> Down from the vault of heaven the starlight dips
> To bathe itself within Love's tearful eyes!
> But he that loves too deeply to be wise
> Crushes Joy's grape and tastes the bitter pips.
> Thus my tormented soul is in eclipse:
> I hear Love calling from the violet skies.
> The fiery waves of ocean rage and roar,
> The daring swimmer takes a mighty bound
> And plunges headlong 'mid the whirling spray.
> The hyacinth is blooming on the shore,
> The faithful heart is bleeding underground,
> A fine red root beneath the human clay!

Oh, Anna, would that as you read this sonnet your soul could be flooded by all the heavenly raptures into which my whole being dissolved when I wrote it down, and when, divinely inspired, I read it aloud afterwards to a group of kindred spirits who are capable of understanding the noblest things in life! Think, oh, think, sweet maid, of your faithful and ecstatic adorer,

AMANDUS VON NEBELSTERN

PS: Forget not, noble maiden, to enclose with your answer a pound of the Virginia tobacco that you grow yourself. It burns very well, and tastes far better than the stuff from Puerto Rico that the other chaps here smoke when they go on a binge.

"Oh, how nice! Oh, how beautiful!" exclaimed Fräulein Ann, pressing the letter to her lips. "And what a lovely poem, with rhymes and everything! Oh, if only I were clever enough to understand it all... But I suppose only an undergraduate could do that. Whatever can that bit about the fine red root mean, I wonder? Why, of course! He's thinking of those long red English carrots – or rapunticas maybe. The darling!"

That very same day, she packed up the tobacco and got the village schoolmaster to sharpen a dozen first-rate goose quills for her, as she wanted to sit down right away and start composing an answer to that wonderful letter.

CHAPTER 1

Incidentally, as she ran out of the kitchen garden, an unmistakable sound of laughter was again heard behind her – and if she had been a tiny bit more observant, she could not have failed to hear a faint little voice crying: "Pull me out! Pull me out! I'm ripe! Ripe! Ripe!"

But, as I said before, she took no notice of it.

2

Containing the first surprising incident, and several other things well worth the reader's attention, which are necessary to the proper development of the narrative.

Herr Dapsul von Zabelthau generally came down from his astronomical tower at midday to join his daughter in a frugal meal, which normally lasted a very short time and was eaten almost in silence, for Dapsul was not at all fond of making conversation. Ann did not say much either, partly out of consideration for him, but mostly because she knew from experience that once Papa really got talking, he said all kinds of weird and unintelligible things that only made her head swim. Today, however, she was so excited about her kitchen garden and the letter from darling Amandus that she kept up a continuous flow of remarks upon both these subjects indiscriminately. Finally, Herr Dapsul von Zabelthau dropped his knife and fork, held both hands to his ears and exclaimed:

"Oh, what stupid, muddled nonsense you do talk!"

Having thus shocked Fräulein Ann into silence, he reverted to the long-winded, tragic style of speech that was characteristic of him.

"My dear daughter," he said, "so far as the vegetables are concerned, I've long been aware that planetary influences this year are peculiarly favourable to such types of garden produce, and that mankind will have its fill of cabbages and radishes and lettuces, thus replenishing its earthy substance and becoming fit to undergo the fire of the world spirit, like a well-fashioned earthen vessel baked in a furnace. The gnomish principle will resist the assaults of the salamander, and I look forward to eating large quantities of parsnips, which you cook extremely well. As for that young gentleman, Amandus von Nebelstern, I haven't the slightest objection to your marrying him as soon as he comes down from the university. Just send up word to me by Gottlieb when you and your fiancé are ready to start for the wedding, and I'll take you over to the church."

Herr Dapsul von Zabelthau paused for a moment or two and then, without noticing the look of rapture on Ann's face, proceeded as follows, smiling and tapping his glass with his fork (the two things always went together with him, but they happened very rarely):

"Your Amandus is a gerundive, one who must and ought to be loved, and I don't mind telling you, my dear Ann, that at a very early date I cast your gerundive's horoscope. In all respects but one the stars are reasonably favourable. He has Jupiter in the ascendant, with Venus in sextile aspect. The only trouble is that the orbit of Sirius passes between them, and precisely at that point there is some great danger, from which he rescues his fiancée. The exact nature of the danger is unfortunately obscure, for some foreign element intervenes, which defies all the efforts of astrology to identify it. But one thing is certain: the power by which Amandus is enabled to effect the rescue in question is that odd psychic condition which is popularly known as folly or stupidity. Oh, my poor daughter!" – at this point Herr Dapsul relapsed into his usual tragic tones – "My poor daughter! I pray that, in spite of all, no sinister power, cunningly concealing itself from my prophetic vision, may suddenly cross your path – that young Amandus von Nebelstern may never have occasion to rescue you from any more serious danger than that of becoming an old maid!"

Herr Dapsul sighed deeply several times, and then continued:

"However, after this danger, the orbit of Sirius suddenly breaks away, and Venus and Jupiter are no longer in opposition, but are reconciled and brought into conjunction."

Herr Dapsul von Zabelthau had not talked so much for years. Feeling thoroughly exhausted, he got up and retired to his observatory.

By the following morning Ann had finished her answer to Amandus's letter. It read as follows:

MY DARLING AMANDUS,

You can't think how glad I was to receive your letter. I've told Papa about it, and he's promised to take us to church for the wedding, so do be quick and come down from the university! I think your poem's absolutely lovely, with all those beautiful rhymes and everything... oh, if only I could understand it properly! When I read it aloud to myself, it all sounds so wonderful that I think I do understand it, but the next moment it's all gone again, everything's vanished into thin air, and I feel as if I'd been reading a lot of words that didn't belong together at all. The schoolmaster says that's bound to happen because it's written in the grand new modern style, but oh dear, I'm such a stupid, ignorant creature! I wonder if I could possibly be an undergraduate for a while without neglecting the farm? Do write and tell me if I could, but I suppose it wouldn't really work. Never mind, once we're married I expect I'll pick up some education from you and get quite used to the modern style. I'm sending you the Virginia tobacco, my dearest Amandykins. I've stuffed my hat box full of it just as much as I could get in, and in the mean time put my straw hat on the Charlemagne that stands in our drawing room – only, of course, he doesn't really stand, because he hasn't got any feet, you know, he's just a bust. Don't laugh at me, Amandykins, but I've written a poem too, and the rhymes are jolly good. Do write and tell me how it is that one knows perfectly well what rhymes with what without being educated or anything. Now, just listen to this:

> I love you, though you're far away,
> And would like to be your wife soon.
> The stars are golden round the moon,
> And the sky is very blue today.
> So you must love me for ever,
> And also hurt me never.
> I'm sending you some Virginia tobacco in great haste,
> And hope it will be to your taste.

You'll have to put up with that for the moment, it's the best I can do, but when I've got to understand the modern style I'll write you something even better. The yellow saxifrage has turned out remarkably well this year, and the beans are coming along nicely, but Fielder – that's my little dachshund – has been given a nasty nip by the big gander: it went right down to the bone! Well, you can't expect everything to be perfect in this world, so with hundreds of kisses, my darling Amandus,

Your faithful fiancée,

ANNA VON ZABELTHAU

PS: I've written all this in a great hurry, that's why some of the letters have got a bit crooked.

PPS: But for goodness' sake don't hold that against me, will you? It's only my writing that's crooked, not me – I'm absolutely straight and on the level and always
>Your faithful
>>ANNA

PPPS: What a lot of things I'd nearly forgotten – aren't I awful? Papa sends his kindest regards, and says you're one who must and ought to be loved, and that you're going to rescue me from some great danger. Well, all I can say is I'm looking forward to it and I remain,
>Yours most affectionately and absolutely faithfully,
>>ANNA VON ZABELTHAU

It was a great load off Ann's mind to have got this letter finished, for she had found it very hard work, and by the time she had addressed the envelope, sealed it, without burning either the paper or her fingers, and handed it and the box of tobacco, on which she had inscribed a fairly legible A.v.N., to Gottlieb with instructions to take them to the town and post them, she was feeling positively light-hearted.

After attending to the needs of the poultry in the courtyard, she dashed off to the place she loved best in all the world: her kitchen garden. When she got to the carrot bed, she decided that the time had come to start catering for the gourmets in the town by taking up the first crop of carrots. Having shouted to the maid to come and help her, Fräulein

CHAPTER 2

Ann stepped cautiously into the very middle of the bed and seized hold of a magnificent specimen. But the moment she started pulling it out, a strange sound was heard.

At this point you are liable to start thinking of mandrakes, and the dreadful, heart-rending shrieks and groans that they utter when dragged out of the earth. But it was not like that at all. The sound that seemed to be coming out of the ground on this occasion was more like faint, joyous laughter.

"Oh!" cried Fräulein Ann in rather a fright, letting go of the plant. "Who's that laughing at me?"

As no further sound was heard, she again seized the plant, which appeared to have shot up higher than all the others, gave it a hearty tug and, taking no notice of the laughter which had started up again, extracted from the soil a most tender and beautiful carrot. But the moment she set eyes on it, she gave a loud shriek of joy and astonishment, which brought the maid dashing up too, and the maid shrieked equally loudly at the marvellous sight that she saw – for round the carrot was a magnificent gold ring with a sparkling topaz in it!

"Why, it must be meant for you!" cried the maid. "It's your wedding ring, Fräulein Ann. You must put it on at once."

"What a silly thing to say!" replied Fräulein Ann. "My wedding ring should come from Herr Amandus von Nebelstern, not from a carrot!"

The more she looked at the ring, the more she liked it. And to tell the truth, the workmanship of this ring seemed far too fine and delicate to have been done by any human being. The hoop consisted of hundreds and hundreds of tiny little figures, arranged in all sorts of different groups. At first sight these figures were almost invisible to the naked eye, but on closer examination they appeared to grow bigger and come to life and dance gracefully about. As for the jewel, it glowed with such extraordinary brilliance that you could hardly have found a match for it even among the topazes in the Green Vault at Dresden.*

"Isn't it beautiful?" said the maid. "It must have been lying under the ground for goodness knows how long. Then it must have got dug up, and the carrot grew through it."

Fräulein Ann now took the ring off the carrot, which, oddly enough, chose this opportunity to slip through her fingers and disappear into the soil. But neither she nor the maid paid much attention to this, as they were far too busy gazing at the wonderful ring, which Fräulein Ann proceeded to place on the little finger of her left hand. As she did so, a sudden stabbing pain shot through that finger, from the base right up to the tip.

Needless to say, when she saw Herr Dapsul von Zabelthau at lunchtime, she told him about this odd experience, and showed him the ring that she had found on the carrot. She then tried to pull it off her finger, so that he could look at it properly, but at this point the stabbing pain started again, and continued as long as she went on pulling. Finally, it became so unbearable that she had to give up.

CHAPTER 2

After examining the ring very carefully *in situ*, Herr Dapsul von Zabelthau made her stretch out her finger and describe all kinds of circles with it in every possible direction. Then he became lost in thought, and without saying another word retired to his tower. But his daughter could hear him sighing and groaning as he mounted the stairs.

Next morning, as Fräulein Ann was tearing round the courtyard in pursuit of a big cockerel who was always making a nuisance of himself, especially by squabbling with the pigeons, Herr Dapsul von Zabelthau emitted such a horrible wail from his megaphone that Ann was quite upset, and, putting her hands to her mouth, she shouted back:

"My dear Papa, what on earth are you making that hideous noise for? You're frightening the poor birds out of their wits!"

"Anna! My daughter, Anna!" yelled Herr Dapsul through the megaphone. "Come up here at once!"

This order came as a great surprise to Fräulein Ann, for Papa had never invited her into the tower before. On the contrary, he had always been very careful to keep the door locked. She could not help feeling rather apprehensive as she climbed up the narrow spiral staircase and opened the heavy door that led into the only room in the tower.

Herr Dapsul von Zabelthau was sitting in a huge armchair of curious design, surrounded by all sorts of weird-looking instruments and dusty volumes. Before him, stretched over a frame on a table, was a sheet of paper on which various lines had been drawn. He had a tall, grey pointed hat on his head, wore flowing robes of grey prunella and had a long white beard on his chin, so that he really looked quite like a wizard. In fact, the false beard prevented Ann from recognizing him at first, and she peered anxiously round the room, wondering where on earth he had got to. But when she realized that the man in the beard was only Papa all the time, she burst into shrieks of laughter.

"Why, Papa! Is it Christmas already?" she asked. "Are you getting into practice for Santa Claus?"

Paying no attention to this remark, Herr Dapsul von Zabelthau picked up a small piece of iron, which he first applied to her forehead and then proceeded to pass several times down her right arm, from the shoulder to the little finger. After that, he made her sit down in the armchair which he had just vacated and place her little finger on the paper stretched over the frame in such a way that the topaz touched the centre from which all the lines radiated. Instantly rays of yellow light shot out from the jewel in all directions, until the whole sheet of paper was coloured deep yellow.

Without taking his eyes off the paper, Herr Dapsul seized a thin plate of metal, raised it with both hands high in the air, and was just about to bring it smashing down onto the paper when he suddenly lost his footing on the slippery stone floor and came down very hard on his bottom, while the metal plate, which he had instinctively let go in order

CHAPTER 2

to break his fall as much as he could and keep the base of his spine intact, went clattering to the ground.

With a faint cry Fräulein Ann emerged from the curious trance-like state into which she had sunk. Herr Dapsul returned, not without difficulty, to the vertical, replaced his grey, conical hat, which had fallen off, rearranged his false beard and sat down opposite Fräulein Ann on a pile of folios.

"My daughter," he said, "my daughter Anna, how did you feel just then? What were you thinking about? What were your sensations? What scenes were being enacted before your mind's eye?"

"Oh, I felt fine," replied Fräulein Ann. "I've never felt better in my life. I was thinking about Herr Amandus von Nebelstern. In fact, he was actually there before my eyes, only he seemed even handsomer than ever, and he was smoking some of that Virginia tobacco I sent him, and he looked absolutely wonderful doing it. Then all at once I felt a tremendous longing for young carrots and fried sausages, and I was terribly pleased when I saw a great dish of them in front of me. I was just going to help myself to some when suddenly there was a horrid sort of jolt and I woke up."

"Amandus von Nebelstern… Virginia tobacco… carrots… sausages…" murmured Herr Dapsul von Zabelthau thoughtfully, motioning his daughter, who was preparing to leave the room, to stay where she was.

"My poor innocent child," he continued, speaking in more tragic tones than ever before, "how lucky you are never to have been initiated into the deep mysteries of the universe, and so to remain unconscious of the dangers that surround you! You know nothing of the supernatural lore of the holy cabbala. Admittedly this disqualifies you from ever participating in the heavenly joys of the wise, who, having reached the very highest stage of development, find it quite unnecessary to eat or drink, except for purposes of pleasure, and are wholly exempt from human limitations. On the other hand, you do not have to endure the anguish of the ascent to that dizzy height, like your unhappy father, who is still far too often overcome by human frailty, whose laborious researches bring him nothing but terror and dismay, and who is still compelled by sheer physical necessity to eat and drink, and generally behave like a human being.

"Know, therefore, my sweet, blissfully ignorant child, that the depths of earth, air, fire and water are crowded with spiritual beings of a higher, and yet more limited nature than Man. There is no need to explain to you, my foolish child, the precise nature of gnomes, salamanders, sylphs and water sprites – you would be quite unable to grasp it if I did. But to give you some indication of the danger that threatens you, let it suffice to say that these spirits aspire to union with human beings, and as they are well aware that human beings are usually most reluctant to contract any such unions, they have all sorts of cunning methods of ensnaring their favourites. To this end, almost anything may serve as a means – a twig, a flower, a glass of water, a flint and steel, or something equally insignificant.

"It is, of course, true that unions of this kind often turn out very satisfactorily, as in the case of the two priests mentioned by the Count of Mirandola,* who were happily married to one such spirit for forty years. It is true, moreover, that some of the greatest sages have sprung from the union of a human being with an elemental spirit. Thus the great Zoroaster was the son of the salamander Oromasis, thus the great Apollonius, the wise Merlin, the brave Count of Cleves and the famous cabbalist, Ben Sira, were the glorious issues of similar marriages and, according to Paracelsus, the beautiful Melusine was in point of fact a sylph. Nevertheless, the danger involved in such unions is only too great, for quite apart from the fact that elemental spirits expect their favourites to be absolute paragons of wisdom, they are also extremely touchy, and quite merciless in avenging insults. For instance, when a certain philosopher who had formed a liaison with a sylph was talking to some friends of his about an attractive lady that he knew, and showing perhaps a shade too much enthusiasm, the sylph instantly displayed in mid-air her own snow-white, shapely leg, as if to convince the friends that she was attractive too, and then killed the poor philosopher on the spot.

"But why do I speak of others? Why don't I speak of myself? I happen to know that a sylph has been in love with me for the last twelve years. But she's too shy to do anything about it, and I feel it would be dangerous for me to make the first advances, as I'm still far too interested in my physical needs to achieve real wisdom. Every morning I make up my mind to fast, and I can quite happily go without breakfast, but when it comes to lunchtime – oh, Anna, my daughter, Anna… you know perfectly well – I make an absolute pig of myself!"

As he spoke these last words, Herr Dapsul von Zabelthau's voice rose almost to a wail, and bitter tears ran down his haggard, sunken cheeks.

"Still," he proceeded more calmly, "I always try to show my appreciation of her kindness by the most scrupulously correct behaviour, the most exquisite courtesy. I never risk smoking a pipe without taking the proper cabbalistic precautions, because I can never tell whether my sensitive air spirit likes that particular brand of tobacco or whether she may not resent the pollution of her element – for which reason it's quite certain that people who smoke Hunting Mixture or Flower of Saxony will never achieve true wisdom or enjoy the love of a sylph. I'm equally careful whenever I'm cutting a piece of hazelwood or picking a flower, or striking a light, because the one thing I want to avoid at all costs is getting on bad terms with an elemental spirit.

"And yet… do you see that nutshell that made me slip and fall over backwards just now, thus ruining the whole experiment, which would otherwise have revealed the secret

CHAPTER 2

of the ring? I don't remember ever eating nuts in this room, which is dedicated exclusively to the pursuit of knowledge – now you know why I always eat my breakfast on the stairs – so it's quite clear that this shell was being used as a hiding place by some little gnome or other, possibly because he wanted to become a student of mine and watch me conducting experiments. For elemental spirits are extremely interested in scientific research, especially if it's the type of thing that the uninitiated regard as crazy or supernatural, and therefore dangerous. That's why they often assist at experiments in animal magnetism. On the other hand, gnomes are very fond of playing practical jokes, and when they find a mesmerist who has not yet reached that highest stage of wisdom which I described a few minutes ago, but is still too much concerned with the physical, it amuses them to put some amorous female of flesh and blood in his arms, just as he's hoping, in a spirit of pure and disinterested passion, to enjoy the embraces of a sylph.

"Well, when I trod on my little student's head just now, he lost his temper and tripped me up. But perhaps he had some more sinister motive for thwarting my efforts to solve the riddle of the ring? Oh, Anna! My daughter, Anna! Listen carefully. My investigations had already gone far enough to show that some gnome had taken a fancy to you, and judging from the nature of the ring, the gnome in question is evidently a man of wealth, breeding and culture. But, my darling Anna, my beloved, sweet, silly little creature, how on earth can a person like you form any sort of alliance with an elemental spirit of that type without grave danger of disaster? If you'd ever read Cassiodorus Remus, you might perhaps reply that on his reliable authority the famous Magdalena de la Cruz,* the abbess of a nunnery at Córdoba in Spain, was happily married to a little gnome for thirty years, and that a young lady called Gertrude, who was a nun at the Convent of Nazareth at Cologne, had a similar experience with a sylph. But just think of the intellectual qualifications of those two pious ladies and compare them with your own. What a difference! Instead of reading books on philosophy, you're frequently to be found feeding hens, geese, ducks and other creatures that the cabbalist finds extremely tiresome. Instead of observing the heavens and watching the stars in their courses, you grub about in the earth. Instead of tracing the pattern of future events in masterly horoscopical projections, you churn milk into butter and make sauerkraut to supply our wretched needs during the winter – though personally I'd be most reluctant to dispense with that particular delicacy. Now I ask you: is that the kind of thing that's likely to appeal in the long run to the delicate sensibilities of a philosophically minded spirit? For the vegetable life of Dapsulheim depends entirely on you, my Anna, and this earthly employment monopolizes your whole attention. And yet, when you found the ring, even when it caused you some sharp twinges of pain, you experienced a wild, delirious joy!

CHAPTER 2

"My recent experiment was an attempt to save you from the power of the ring, to free you from the influence of the gnome who is trying to ensnare you. The experiment failed because of that naughty little student in the nutshell. And yet... I feel an urge, such as I've never felt before, to do battle with this spirit. After all, you are my child. Admittedly, your poor mother was neither a sylph nor a salamander, nor any other type of elemental spirit. She was merely a country girl of good family, who was rudely referred to in the neighbourhood as the 'Goat Girl', on account of her pastoral tastes – for every day she used to pasture a pretty little flock of white goats on the green hillside, whilst I, lovesick fool that I was, serenaded her from my tower on a recorder. Still, you are and always will be my child, my own flesh and blood. I will save you! This mystic file shall free you here and now from the accursed power of the ring!"

So saying, Herr Dapsul von Zabelthau picked up a small file and started filing away at the ring. But he had hardly begun to do so before Fräulein Ann gave a loud scream of pain.

"Papa! Papa!" she cried. "You're filing my finger off!"

True enough, thick dark blood was pouring out from under the ring.

Herr Dapsul dropped the file, sank half-fainting into the armchair and gave a cry of despair.

"Oh! Oh! Oh!" he wailed. "Now I've done it! At any moment now, the gnome will appear in a rage and bite my head off, if the sylph doesn't come to my rescue! Oh, Anna! Anna! Go away before it's too late!"

Fräulein Ann, who had been finding Papa's conversation rather a strain and wanting to get away for some time, disappeared like lightning down the stairs.

3

*How a curious individual arrived at
Dapsulheim, and what happened then.*

Herr Dapsul von Zabelthau had just tearfully embraced his daughter and was about to go upstairs to his study, where he expected at any moment to receive a dreadful visitation from the angry gnome, when a shrill, merry bugle call was heard, and into the courtyard sprang a tiny man on horseback, whose appearance was really rather out of the ordinary. His yellow horse was not very tall, and of slender and elegant build, so that in spite of his disproportionately large head the little man did not look at all like a dwarf, for he positively towered above the horse's neck. This was wholly attributable, however, to the length of his trunk, for the legs and feet that hung over the saddle were so small as to be hardly worth being called so. For the rest, the little fellow wore a most becoming costume of golden-yellow satin, a tall hat of the same material with a huge grass-green plume in it and riding boots of beautifully polished mahogany.

With a shrill "Whoa!" he came to a halt immediately in front of Herr Dapsul von Zabelthau. He made as if to dismount, then suddenly, quick as lightning, shot under the horse's belly and leapt two or three times into the air on the other side to the height of about twelve feet, turning half a dozen somersaults in the course of every foot, and finally coming to rest upside down with his head on the saddle. In this position he started galloping forwards, backwards and sideways, and executing all sorts of curious twists and turns, while his feet tapped out trochees, pyrrhics, dactyls and other metrical rhythms in the air. When the pretty little equestrian acrobat finally came to a standstill and made a courtly bow, the following words were seen to be inscribed on the floor of the courtyard: "Kindest regards to you and your daughter, my dear Herr Dapsul von Zabelthau". The message was written, or rather ridden, in beautiful Roman uncials.

The little man now leapt down from his horse, turned three cartwheels and announced that the Right Honourable Baron Porphyrio von Ockerodastes, otherwise known as Corduanspitz, sent his compliments to Herr Dapsul von Zabelthau, and if it would be convenient to Herr Dapsul, the baron would like to come and stay with him for a few days, as he hoped very soon to become his next-door neighbour.

Herr Dapsul von Zabelthau looked more dead than alive as he stood there, rigid with terror, clutching his daughter's arm for support. With a great effort his trembling lips managed to frame the words:

"D-d-delighted, I'm s-s-sure."

CHAPTER 3

No sooner had he made this reply than with the same formalities as those which had marked his arrival the tiny horseman departed.

"Oh, my daughter!" wailed Herr Dapsul von Zabelthau, sobbing and snivelling. "Oh, my daughter, my poor unhappy daughter! It's only too obvious that it's the gnome who's coming – to carry you off and wring my neck! But we must summon up all our courage – that is, if we've got any left. It may conceivably be possible to appease the elemental spirit's wrath – only, we must do our very best to ensure that our conduct towards him is scrupulously correct. Just a moment, my dear child, and I'll read you a few chapters of Lactantius or St Thomas Aquinas* on the proper way to behave with elemental spirits, so that you don't make some horrible faux pas."

But before Herr Dapsul von Zabelthau could lay his hands on Lactantius or St Thomas Aquinas or any other authority on elemental etiquette, some music was heard approaching, rather like the noise produced by children with a good-enough ear to go carol-singing at Christmas. A magnificent procession was coming up the road. It was led by about sixty or seventy tiny men on tiny yellow horses, all dressed, like the messenger, in yellow costumes, pointed hats and polished mahogany boots. Behind them came a carriage made of the purest crystal, drawn by eight yellow horses and followed by about forty other carriages of less imposing appearance, some with six horses and some with four.

There were also great numbers of gorgeously dressed pages, footmen and other servants swarming about everywhere, and altogether it was a very cheerful and unusual sight.

Herr Dapsul von Zabelthau stood lost in gloomy wonder, but Fräulein Ann, who had never before suspected that the world contained anything so neat and pretty as these miniature people and horses, was so overjoyed that she forgot about everything else. For instance, having opened her mouth wide to let out a cry of delight, she forgot to shut it again.

The eight-horse carriage stopped immediately in front of Herr Dapsul von Zabelthau. Postilions sprang down from their horses, pages and footmen came hurrying up, the carriage door was opened, and out of the carriage, respectfully assisted by many willing hands, stepped Baron Porphyrio von Ockerodastes, otherwise known as Corduanspitz.

So far as his figure was concerned, the baron bore no resemblance whatever to the *Apollo Belvedere* – nor even to the *Dying Gladiator*.* For quite apart from the fact that he was barely three feet tall, a third of his diminutive person consisted of his head, which was obviously much too big for him, and was embellished with a huge, long, hooked nose and a pair of great, round, protuberant eyes. As his trunk was also rather long, there was only about four inches left for his legs and feet. However, good use had been made of the space available, for considered in themselves the baronial nether limbs were as elegant as one could hope to see. On the other hand, they were apparently not quite strong enough to carry the weight of that noble head, for the baron had a rather stumbling gait and was constantly falling down, but whenever this happened, he immediately popped up again like a jack-in-the-box, so that these falls of his seemed like deliberate features of a rather graceful dance. He wore a tight-fitting costume of glittering gold brocade, and a hat that looked almost like a crown, with an enormous plume of cabbage-green feathers in it.

The moment the baron reached the ground, he rushed up to Herr Dapsul von Zabelthau and seized both his hands. Then he jumped up and flung his arms round his neck, and, while suspended from it, exclaimed in a deep, booming voice, such as one would never have expected to proceed from a person of his size: "Oh, my dear Dapsul von Zabelthau – my beloved father-in-law!" After that, he hopped nimbly down and ran, or rather hurled himself, towards Fräulein Ann. Seizing the hand with the ring on it, he covered it with loud smacking kisses and exclaimed in the same booming tones as before: "Oh, my beautiful Fräulein Anna von Zabelthau, my darling fiancée!"

Then the baron clapped his hands, and immediately the shrill, noisy, childish music started up again, whereupon more than a hundred tiny gentlemen descended from the carriages and horses and began dancing as the messenger had done, sometimes on their heads and sometimes on their feet, in the prettiest trochaic, spondaic, iambic, pyrrhic, anapaestic, tribrachic, bacchiac, anti-bacchiac, choriambic and dactylic rhythms, so that it was quite a pleasure to watch them.

Fräulein Ann, however, was in no position to enjoy it, for, as soon as she had recovered from the shock the baron's words had given her, she started worrying – as well she might – about some problems of domestic economy.

"How can I possibly find room," she thought, "for all these little creatures in a small house like ours? Perhaps, in the circumstances, it would be all right to make the servants sleep in the big barn – but will there be room for them even there, I wonder? And what on earth am I to do with all the gentlemen in the carriages? They're probably used to very grand bedrooms and soft, comfortable beds. If I moved the two cart horses out of the stable, and if I had the heart to turn the old lame bay mare out to grass – even so, I wonder if there'd be enough room for all the tiny horses that the ugly little baron has brought with him. And then, what about the forty-one carriages? But that's not the worst of it by any means! Why, good Lord, it'll take more than a whole year's supply of food to satisfy all these little creatures even for a couple of days!"

It was this last consideration that really upset her. She saw everything disappearing – all the young vegetables, all the mutton, all the poultry and salted beef, even the beetroot brandy – and the very idea of it brought bitter tears to her eyes. Moreover, she seemed to detect a positively insolent, gloating expression on Baron Corduanspitz's face, and this gave her courage, while his followers were still dancing away for all they were worth, to tell him bluntly that much as her father might welcome his visit, it was quite out of the question for him to remain at Dapsulheim for more than a couple of hours, since there was a total lack of space and of all the other things that would be necessary for the reception and proper entertainment of a rich and distinguished visitor like himself, together with all his suite.

At this, little Corduanspitz suddenly became as sweet as sugar. He pressed Fräulein Ann's rather rough and not particularly white hand to his lips, closing his eyes as he did so, and assured her that the very last thing he wished to do was to cause the slightest inconvenience to her dear papa or to his charming daughter. He had brought with him everything that would be needed in the way of food and wine – and as for accommodation, all he asked was a little bit of ground out of doors, where his servants could erect his usual travelling palace, in which he and his whole entourage would spend their visit, livestock and all.

Fräulein Ann was so delighted by this information that, in order to show how generous she could be, even with her choicest delicacies, she was just going to offer the little man one of the doughnuts that she had saved from the village fair and a glass of beetroot brandy, unless he would prefer some of the stout that the housemaid had brought back from the town and had recommended as a tonic. But at that moment Corduanspitz added that the most suitable site for the palace would appear to be the kitchen garden – and all Ann's cheerfulness evaporated.

The baron's entourage continued to celebrate their master's arrival at Dapsulheim by holding their own kind of Olympic Games, which included such items as knocking one another over backwards by running their big heads against one another's protuberant stomachs, flinging themselves high into the air and playing games of skittles in which the players acted as bowlers, bowls and skittles indiscriminately. Meanwhile, the tiny Baron Porphyrio von Ockerodastes was deeply engaged with Herr Dapsul von Zabelthau in a conversation which seemed to be growing more serious every moment, until at last they went off hand in hand and climbed up into the observatory.

Feeling very worried and frightened, Fräulein Ann dashed off to the kitchen garden, in the hope of saving something out of the wreck. The housemaid was there already, staring straight in front of her with her mouth open, and standing absolutely motionless, as if she had been turned into a pillar of salt, like Lot's wife.* Fräulein Ann froze into a state of equal immobility beside her. Finally, they both uttered a simultaneous scream, which rose echoing to the sky:

"My goodness gracious, what an awful thing to happen!"

The whole kitchen garden had become a wilderness. Not a single cabbage sprouted, not a single lettuce bloomed. The place was like an area of devastation.

CHAPTER 3

"Why, it's those dratted little creatures!" cried the housemaid in a rage. "No one else could have done it. Travel in carriages, do they? Trying to pretend they're gentry, I suppose! The idea! Goblins, that's what they are, Fräulein Ann, you can take my word for it. It's nothing but a lot of black magic, and I wish to goodness I'd got a boxwood cross on me, then they'd soon see what would happen! But just let me get at them, the little beasts! I'll squash them all flat with this spade!"

So saying, the housemaid brandished her formidable weapon in the air, while Fräulein Ann sobbed loudly.

Just then, they were approached by four gentlemen on Corduanspitz's staff, who had such a delightful air of elegance and made such courtly bows, and looked so extraordinarily odd into the bargain, that instead of knocking them down as she had intended, the housemaid slowly lowered her spade, and Fräulein Ann stopped crying.

The gentlemen introduced themselves as the baron's closest friends, though it was obvious from their clothes that they were of four different nationalities. They gave their names as Pan Kapustowicz of Poland, Herr von Schwarzrettig of Pomerania, Signor di Broccoli of Italy and Monsieur de Rocambole of France,* and announced in the most magniloquent phraseology that the workmen would be arriving at any moment, and that the charming young lady would then have the pleasure of watching the inconceivably rapid erection of a beautiful palace of pure silk.

"What's the good of a silk palace to me?" cried Fräulein Ann, bursting into tears again. "What do I care for your Baron Corduanspitz anyway? You've gone off with all my lovely vegetables, you wicked creatures – and I'll never be happy again!"

They comforted her, however, by the assurance that they were in no way responsible for the devastation of the kitchen garden – that on the contrary it would soon be restored to a state of such abundant fertility as she had never seen before in it or any other kitchen garden in the world.

The tiny workmen did indeed arrive, and now such a frantic riot of confused activity broke loose all over the garden that Fräulein Ann and the housemaid ran panic-stricken behind a bush, where they stood waiting to see what would happen next. How exactly it was done, they had no idea, for there was evidently something rather queer about it, but in a very few minutes a tall and splendid pavilion of some golden-yellow material had taken shape before their eyes, adorned with many-coloured plumes and streamers, and occupying the whole area of the big kitchen garden, so that the guy ropes had to go right over the village to the wood beyond, where they were made fast to some trees.

The erection of the pavilion had hardly been completed before Baron Porphyrio von Ockerodastes came down from the observatory with Herr Dapsul von Zabelthau, embraced him several times, climbed into the eight-horse carriage and, accompanied by his whole suite, in the same order as before, drove into the silken palace, which closed behind the last member of the procession.

Fräulein Ann had never seen Papa looking like this before. Every trace of his usual gloom had been wiped off his face. He looked almost as if he was smiling, and there was something positively radiant about his expression, as though he had quite unexpectedly found himself floating in a great sea of happiness.

Without saying a word, Herr Dapsul von Zabelthau took Fräulein Ann by the hand, led her into the house, embraced her three times in rapid succession and finally burst out:

"Oh, lucky Anna! Lucky, lucky child! And lucky father! Oh, my dear daughter, all our anxieties, all our sorrows, all our afflictions are now over! A lot has fallen to you which is not often granted to a mortal woman. You must know that this Baron Porphyrio von Ockerodastes, otherwise known as Corduanspitz, is very far from being a malignant gnome, although he is descended from one such elemental spirit, for the ancestor in question succeeded, under the tuition of the salamander Oromasis, in purifying his better nature. Having thus been purged by fire, he aspired to the love of a mortal woman, married her and became the founder of the most illustrious line that has ever honoured parchment with the record of its names.

"I believe I've already told you, my daughter Anna, that this pupil of the great salamander Oromasis, the famous gnome Tsilmenech – a Chaldean name which means much the same as 'blockhead' in our language – fell in love with the celebrated Magdalena de la Cruz, the abbess of a convent at Córdoba, or Cordova, in Spain, and was happily married to her for about thirty years. Well, my dear friend, Baron Porphyrio von Ockerodastes, is descended from the glorious race of higher beings that resulted from this union, and has adopted the name Corduanspitz in order to distinguish himself from a prouder, but in reality less distinguished, collateral line, which bears the name of Morocco. For the addition of the 'spitz', or 'spike', to the 'Corduan', or 'Cordovan', there must be some special elemental or astrological explanation, but I've not as yet had time to work it out.

"Well, following the example of his ancestor, the gnome Tsilmenech, who fell in love with Magdalena de la Cruz when she was only twelve years old, the excellent Ockerodastes has been one of your admirers ever since you reached the same age. He was lucky enough to get hold of a small gold ring of yours, and now you're wearing his ring too, so you're irrevocably engaged to marry him."

"What?" cried Fräulein Ann in horror. "What? Marry *him*? Am I supposed to marry that revolting little goblin? But I'm engaged to marry Herr Amandus von Nebelstern, and have been for ages! No, no, a thousand times no! I *won't* have that ugly little creature as my husband, no matter where he comes from or what he's made of, cordovan or morocco!"*

CHAPTER 3

"In that case," replied Herr Dapsul von Zabelthau in sterner tones, "in that case, I am sorry to see that your invincibly earthy soul is quite impervious to heavenly wisdom. So you call that noble elemental spirit, Porphyrio von Ockerodastes, ugly and revolting – doubtless because he is only three feet tall, and apart from his fine great head has nothing very substantial in the way of arms, legs or other minor details – instead of realizing that an earth spirit who cares about his appearance, as you may be sure he does, simply can't afford to have very long legs, for fear of getting them tangled up with his coat-tails. Oh, my poor daughter, how hopelessly wrong you are! All beauty consists in wisdom, all wisdom consists in thought, and the physical symbol of thought is the head. The more head, the more beauty and wisdom, and if only Man could reject all the other parts of the body as pernicious luxuries, he would become a real paragon! For what is the origin of all the trouble and misfortune, of all the strife and discord – in short, of all the things that spoil our earthly life? The damnable bodily appetites! Oh, how calm, how peaceful, how happy this world would be if only human beings could exist without trunk, buttocks, arms or legs – if they consisted of nothing but busts! That's why it is such a good idea to represent great statesmen and scholars by busts, thus symbolizing the higher nature which they evidently possess – or how could they have attained such eminence or written so many books? And so, my daughter Anna, let's hear no such words as 'ugly' or 'revolting' applied to that noblest of spirits, the glorious Porphyrio von Ockerodastes, whose fiancée you are and will continue to be.

"You must know that your father also is soon to reach that state of ideal happiness to which he has so long aspired in vain. Porphyrio von Ockerodastes has been informed of the fact that the sylph Nehalilah – a Syrian word which may be roughly translated 'Sharp-Nose' – has fallen in love with me, and he has promised to help me in every way he can to become worthy of an alliance with that sublime spiritual being. I'm sure you'll like your future stepmother very much, my dear child. May we have the good fortune to celebrate both our marriages in one and the same happy hour!"

As he spoke these last words, Herr Dapsul von Zabelthau gave his daughter a meaningful look, and then with an air of pathos left the room.

Fräulein Ann's spirits sank very low as she remembered that a long time ago, when she was still a child, a small gold ring had in some unaccountable way slipped off her finger and got lost. It was now only too clear that the horrid little magician had lured her into a trap from which it was almost impossible to escape, and she felt absolutely miserable about it. Her misery demanded some immediate outlet, so she seized a goose quill and wrote to Herr Amandus von Nebelstern as follows:

CHAPTER 3

MY DARLING AMANDUS,

Everything's gone wrong. I'm the most miserable person in the world, and I'm crying such bucketfuls of tears that even the animals feel sorry for me, so you'll feel even sorrier. Actually, it concerns you just as much as me, so you're bound to be every bit as miserable as I am. Anyway, you know we love each other like anything and I'm your fiancée and Father was going to take us to church for the wedding? Well, all of a sudden a nasty little yellow man turns up in an eight-horse carriage with hundreds of gentlemen and servants all dressed up and says I've exchanged rings with him and we're engaged to be married! And just imagine, the awful thing is that Papa says the same thing! He says I must marry the little beast because he comes from a very grand family. Well, maybe he does, considering the number of people he's brought with him and the gorgeous clothes they wear, but he's got such a ghastly name that it would be quite enough in itself to put me off marrying him. It's made up of a lot of heathen words that I can't even pronounce properly. By the way, he's also called Corduanspitz, but that's only his surname. Do write and tell me if the Corduanspitzes are really as grand and famous as all that – I expect people in the town will know. I simply can't think what's come over Papa in his old age – he's going to get married again, and that ugly little Corduanspitz is fixing things up for him with a woman who goes floating about in the air. Heaven help us if he does! The housemaid shrugs her shoulders and says she doesn't think much of ladies who float about in the air or swim about in the water – she'll give notice at once, and she only hopes for my sake that my stepmama breaks her neck the first time she goes joy-riding on Walpurgis Night. Fine goings-on, I must say! But you're my only hope. I know you're the one who must and ought to be loved, and who's going to rescue me from a great danger. Well, this is it, so come as fast as you can to the rescue of

Yours till death do us part,

Yours miserably but faithfully,

ANNA VON ZABELTHAU

PS: Couldn't you challenge that little yellow man to a duel? You'd be sure to win, for he's rather wobbly on his legs.

PPS: Please, please get dressed at once and hurry to the rescue of

Your most unhappy but, as aforesaid, most faithful fiancée,

ANNA VON ZABELTHAU

4

*A description of a mighty monarch's
court, followed by an account of a duel,
and other unusual incidents.*

Fräulein Ann felt absolutely paralysed with misery. She was sitting with her arms crossed, staring out of the window and paying no attention whatever to the cackling and crowing and chirping and clucking of the fowls in the courtyard, who, now that it was beginning to get dark, expected her to come and put them to bed as usual. She even accepted the situation with complete indifference, when the maid did the job instead and gave her pet cockerel, who refused to yield to the inevitable and tried to rebel against his mistress's deputy, quite a sharp cut with her whip. The pangs of love that were racking her heart made her quite insensible to the sufferings of her dear little ward, to whose upbringing she had devoted many a pleasant hour, although she had never read Lord Chesterfield or Knigge, and had not even consulted Madame de Genlis* or any other authority on the technique of education – which may perhaps be regarded as rather thoughtless of her.

Corduanspitz had not been seen all day, but had remained closeted with Herr Dapsul von Zabelthau in the tower, where some very important business was doubtless being transacted. Just then, however, Fräulein Ann noticed the little man staggering across the courtyard in the glow of the setting sun. In his bright-yellow clothes she thought he looked nastier than ever, and the funny way he had of hopping along, falling down one moment and shooting up again the next, which would have made any other girl laugh herself sick, only made her feel all the more wretched. In fact, she finally held both hands in front of her face in order to shut out the loathsome spectacle.

Suddenly she felt something tugging at her apron.

"Down, Fielder!" she cried, thinking it was her dog. But it was not the dog. For when she took her hands away from her face, there was Baron Porphyrio von Ockerodastes, who now leapt with extraordinary agility onto her lap and flung both his arms round her neck.

Fräulein Ann gave a shriek of terror and disgust, and jumped up from her chair. But Corduanspitz remained suspended from her neck, and suddenly became frightfully heavy, so that poor Ann felt as if she was carrying at least a ton, and swift as an arrow shot back into her seat. As she did so, he slipped off her lap, lowered himself onto his small right knee with all the grace and courtesy that a certain lack of equilibrium from which he suffered would allow and, speaking in a clear, rather peculiar but not exactly unpleasant voice, expressed himself as follows:

CHAPTER 4

"My adorable Fräulein Anna von Zabelthau, my splendid young lady, my most eligible fiancée, don't be angry – I beg you, I beseech you! Don't be angry, please don't be angry! I know you think my servants have ruined your beautiful kitchen garden in order to build my palace, but (oh, ye powers of the universe!) if only you could look inside my small body and see the loving, generous heart that beats there – if only you could perceive all the cardinal virtues that are assembled in my bosom beneath this yellow satin! Oh, how foreign to my nature is the shameful cruelty of which you accuse me! How could a gentle monarch possibly do such a thing to his own subj— But stop, stop! What are mere words, mere phrases? You must see it all for yourself, my dear. Yes, you must see for yourself the glories that await you. You must come with me, come with me this very moment! I'll conduct you to my palace, where a joyful people is impatient for the arrival of its master's beloved bride!"

You can imagine how horrified Ann felt at this proposal, how reluctant she was to go a single step with the dreadful little monster. But Corduanspitz went on describing the extraordinary beauty, the boundless riches of the kitchen garden, which he called his "palace", so convincingly that in the end she decided just to go and have a peep into the pavilion, as that could not possibly do her any harm.

The little fellow was so overjoyed that he turned at least twelve cartwheels in rapid succession. Then very politely he took Fräulein Ann's hand and led her through the garden to the palace of silk.

"Oh!" cried Fräulein Ann, and stood rooted to the spot when the hangings across the entrance were rolled up, revealing an immense kitchen garden of such beauty as she had never seen, even in her wildest dreams, of blooming cabbages and cauliflowers – for every conceivable variety of cauliflower and cabbage and carrot and lettuce and pea and bean was blooming and flourishing there in such glittering splendour that the whole effect was quite indescribable.

The music of fifes and drums and cymbals now rose to a crescendo, and the four polite gentlemen whom Fräulein Ann had already got to know – namely Herr Schwarzrettig, Monsieur de Rocambole, Signor di Broccoli and Pan Kapustowicz – came forwards with many ceremonious gestures of respect.

"My Gentlemen of the Bedchamber," explained Porphyrio von Ockerodastes with a smile, and, preceded by the same gentlemen, he led Fräulein Ann between two ranks of red-coated English carrot guards to the middle of the garden, where a splendid throne rose high into the air. Around this throne were assembled the great dignitaries of the kingdom: the lettuce princes with the bean princesses, the cucumber dukes with the prince of melons at their head, the secretary of state for the cauliflowers, the general staff of the onion and carrot forces, the dames commanders of the cabbage empire, and so on, all dressed in gorgeous clothes appropriate to their ranks and stations. And in and out among them ran about a hundred lavender and fennel pageboys, scattering perfume as they went.

When Ockerodastes had mounted the throne with Fräulein Ann, Lord High Chamberlain Turnips made a sign with his long baton, and immediately the music stopped and everyone stood listening in respectful silence. Then Ockerodastes lifted up his voice and spoke very solemnly as follows:

"My loyal and very dear subjects! Behold at my side the noble Fräulein Anna von Zabelthau, whom I have chosen to be my consort. Endowed with every virtue, every charm, she has long watched over you like a loving mother – nay, more: prepared soft, rich beds for you, and tended and fostered you in every way. You will find her, and will always continue to find her, an exemplary queen. Now signify, by three orderly cheers, your respectful acknowledgement of the benefit that I am graciously pleased to bestow upon you."

At a second sign from Lord High Chamberlain Turnips, a thousand voices were now raised in a cheer, the onion artillery fired off a salute, and the band of the carrot guards played the well-known national anthem: 'Lettuce, Lettuce and Green Parsley!' It was a truly sublime moment, which brought tears to the eyes of all the aristocracy, but especially of the dames commanders of the cabbage empire. As for Fräulein Ann, her emotion became almost uncontrollable when she noticed that the little man was wearing a crown of sparkling diamonds on his head and carrying a golden sceptre.

"Ooh!" she cried. "My goodness gracious! I'd no idea you were such an important person, my dear Herr von Corduanspitz!"

"My darling Anna," replied Ockerodastes, speaking very quietly, "circumstances compelled me to introduce myself to your father under an assumed name. As a matter of fact, my dear child, I'm a very powerful king, and it's impossible to say how vast my kingdom is, for the simple reason that no one has ever bothered to mark its boundaries on a map. It is the King of Vegetables, Daucus Carota the First, my sweetest Anna, who offers you his hand and his crown. All vegetable princes are my vassals – except that, in accordance with a time-honoured custom, the King of Beans governs my kingdom for one day in every year."

"Do you mean to say," asked Fräulein Ann delightedly, "do you mean to say I'm going to be a queen, and this wonderful, glorious kitchen garden will belong to me?"

King Daucus Carota assured her once more that such would indeed be the case, and added that every single vegetable that grew out of the soil would be subject to his and her jurisdiction.

Now, Fräulein Ann had never expected anything quite like this, and since his transformation into King Daucus Carota the First, she found that little Corduanspitz was not nearly so ugly as before, and that his crown and sceptre and royal robes suited him uncommonly well. When she took into consideration his beautiful manners and the wealth that such a marriage would bring her, she could not help feeling that she was in a position to make a far better match than any other country girl in the world – for there she was, all of a sudden, engaged to marry a king!

She was so delighted at the prospect that she asked her royal fiancé if she could move into his beautiful palace right away and get married the following morning – to which King Daucus replied that, charmed as he was by her enthusiasm, circumstances made it necessary to postpone his happiness a little longer. For one thing, it was absolutely essential that Herr Dapsul von Zabelthau should not learn his future son-in-law's real identity just yet, as such knowledge might interfere with the processes designed to bring about his union with the sylph Nehalilah. For another, he had assured Herr Dapsul that both weddings should take place on the same day.

So Fräulein Ann promised not to tell her father anything about it, after which she left the palace of silk amid the uproarious cheers of the populace, who were intoxicated with joy at her beauty and at her gracious, condescending manner.

That night, in a dream she revisited the kingdom of her darling King Daucus Carota, and floated in a sea of bliss.

The letter that she had sent to Herr Amandus von Nebelstern had produced a terrible effect on the poor young man, and it was not long before she received the following answer:

MY HEAVENLY ANNA, IDOL OF MY HEART,

Every word in your letter was a dagger, a sharp, red-hot, envenomed, deadly dagger that pierced my heart. Oh, Anna! Are you to be torn from my arms? What a dreadful thought! I still do not understand why I did not go mad on the spot and make a terrible scene. However, raging against my cruel destiny, I fled the haunts of men, and, directly after lunch, instead of playing billiards as I normally do, I rushed out into the woods, where I wrung my hands and a thousand times invoked your name. It started pouring with rain, and I had just put on a brand-new red velvet cap with a splendid gold tassel. I am told that I have never had a cap that suited me so well. The rain was liable to spoil this triumph of taste, but what does a despairing lover care for caps, or velvet, or gold? I wandered about until I was absolutely soaked and frozen stiff, and had got frightful indigestion. This drove me into a nearby public house, where I had some excellent mulled claret and smoked a pipe of your heavenly Virginia tobacco. Then I felt the promptings of divine inspiration, so I whipped out my notebook and dashed off a dozen glorious poems – and all at once, thanks to the marvellous power of poesy, I found that both my pains had disappeared, not only the pangs of despairing love, but the pangs of indigestion also. Of these poems I need only show you the last, and your heart will be filled like mine with joy and hope, O model of maidenhood.

CHAPTER 4

> I writhe in ghastly pain;
> Love's candles no more rain
> Their light upon my brain;
> To smile I strive in vain.
> But soon my downcast mind
> Apt words and rhymes doth find.
> Quickly I write them down,
> And straightway cease to frown.
> Love's candles once more rain
> Comfort upon my brain.
> Forgotten is my pain,
> And I can smile again.

Yes, my sweet Anna, I shall soon hasten, like some knight errant, to your side and deliver you from the miscreant who is trying to wrest you from me. To save you from despair, in the mean time I am transcribing for your benefit a few divinely consoling aphorisms from the treasury of my excellent tutor. You can feast upon them until I arrive in person.

> Your bosom swells, your soul is growing wings?
> Let heart and mind do even odder things!

> Love can turn to hate,
> If it comes too late.

Love is a flower, a sun that cannot set:
Wash well behind the ears, but don't get wet!

In winter, you say, the wind blows chill?
Then wear a warm coat, or you're sure to be ill!

What divine, sublime, exuberantly pregnant maxims they are! And how simply, how unpretentiously, how pithily expressed! So once more, my sweetest maiden, be comforted, and cherish me as ever in your heart. I am coming to you; I will save you; I will press you to the loving, tempestuously heaving bosom of
>Your faithful
>>AMANDUS VON NEBELSTERN

PS: Under no circumstances can I challenge Herr von Corduanspitz to a duel. You see, my Anna, every drop of blood that might flow from your Amandus by reason of the deadly onslaught of an insolent foe would be the precious lifeblood of poesy, the ichor of the gods, which must on no account be spilt. The world has a right to expect a man like me to take good care of himself, and do all he can to preserve himself for posterity.

The poet's sword is his pen. I will attack my rival with Tyrtaean war songs,* run him through with pointed epigrams, cut him down with dithyrambs full of passionate love. Such are the poet's true weapons – which, eternally triumphant, secure him against every assault – and thus armed and accoutred I shall appear and do battle for your hand, my Anna!

Farewell… once more I press you to my breast! Put all your trust in my love, and more especially in my heroic temper, which will shrink from no danger that may be involved in releasing you from the shameful toils into which a fiendish monster has apparently enticed you.

When Fräulein Ann got this letter, she was having a game of tag with her fiancé, King Daucus Carota the First, in the meadow at the bottom of the garden, and deriving great amusement from suddenly ducking down when running at full speed, and seeing the little king go flying over her head. Contrary to her usual habit, she stuffed her lover's screed into her pocket unopened, for, as we shall soon see, it had come too late.

Herr Dapsul von Zabelthau simply could not make out why Fräulein Ann had suddenly changed her mind and taken such a liking to Herr Porphyrio von Ockerodastes, whom she had found so repulsive at first. He consulted the stars about it, but as they could not produce any satisfactory explanation either, he was forced to the conclusion that the mind of Man is more unfathomable than any other mystery of the universe, and quite beyond the scope of astrological interpretation.

He could not believe that Fräulein Ann had come to love her fiancé purely on account of his higher nature, for the little fellow was completely devoid of physical beauty – and although, as the gentle reader will have observed, Herr Dapsul von Zabelthau's idea of beauty differed widely from that of the average young girl, he had still had enough experience of life on this earth to know that the said young girl is far more interested in the outside of the house than in such respectable tenants as intelligence, common sense, imagination or good nature, and that a man who does not look well in a fashionable tailcoat, even if he is a Shakespeare, a Goethe, a Tieck or a Friedrich Richter,* has no chance against a lieutenant of hussars with a reasonably good figure and a becoming uniform, once he takes it into his head to make advances to a girl.

Admittedly, in the case of Fräulein Ann things had turned out rather differently, and neither beauty nor intelligence had been the deciding factor. Still, it is really most unusual for a poor country girl to be suddenly transformed into a queen, and under the circumstances Herr Dapsul von Zabelthau could hardly be expected to guess the truth, especially as the stars had let him down.

You can imagine how harmonious relations now became between these three – Herr Porphyrio, Herr Dapsul and Fräulein Ann – so much so that Herr Dapsul emerged from his study far oftener than he had ever done before, to hold all sorts of delightful conversations with his future son-in-law, and in particular developed the habit of having his breakfast downstairs in the house. At the same hour,

CHAPTER 4

Herr Porphyrio von Ockerodastes would leave his palace of silk and allow Fräulein Ann to feed him with bread and butter.

"My goodness!" she often giggled into his ear. "My goodness, if only Papa knew that you're really a king, darling Corduanspitz!"

"Steady now, dearest heart," Daucus Carota would reply. "Steady now, dearest heart, and don't let your feelings run away with you. The happy day is rapidly approaching."

One morning, the schoolmaster presented Fräulein Ann with a delicious bunch of radishes from his garden. The gift was particularly welcome, for Herr Dapsul von Zabelthau was extremely fond of radishes, but Ann could not get any from her own kitchen garden, where the palace had been built. Moreover, it suddenly occurred to her for the first time that among all the various vegetables in the palace she had not noticed a single radish.

Having quickly washed the radishes that she had been given, she served them up to her father for breakfast. Herr Dapsul von Zabelthau had already gobbled up most of them, after mercilessly lopping off their leaves and dipping them in the salt cellar, when Corduanspitz came in.

"My dear Ockerodastes, do have some radishes!" was Herr Dapsul von Zabelthau's greeting. One large and particularly handsome radish still remained on the dish. But the moment Corduanspitz caught sight of it, his eyes started flashing with rage, and he burst out in a terrible roar:

"What? Perfidious duke, do you dare to appear again before my eyes? Nay, have you the shameless effrontery to force your way into a house that is under my protection? Have I not banished you for all eternity for presuming to dispute my rightful claim to the throne? Away, away with you, traitorous vassal!"

The radish had suddenly developed two tiny legs beneath its huge head, and with these it immediately leapt out of the dish, strutted up to Corduanspitz, and delivered itself as follows:

"Cruel Daucus Carota the First, it is in vain that you attempt to exterminate my race. Has any member of your species ever boasted as large a head as I and my kinsmen have? Intelligence, wisdom, prudence, courtesy, with all these qualities we are endowed, and whereas you spend your time hanging about kitchens and stables, and are only valued in the prime of youth, so that your fleeting charms are quite literally *la beauté du diable de la jeunesse*,* we enjoy the society of the upper classes, and are greeted with delight the moment we so much as raise our green heads above the soil. Daucus Carota, I defy you, hulking great brute though you are, like all your tribe! Let us see which of us is the stronger!"

With these words the Duke of Radishes started brandishing a long whip, and without further parley sprang to the attack of King Daucus Carota the First. The latter instantly drew his tiny sword and defended himself manfully. The two

CHAPTER 4

little creatures went scuffling round the room in a series of extraordinary leaps and bounds, until at last Daucus Carota got his opponent so effectually cornered that he was compelled to take a flying jump through the open window and make off at full speed. King Daucus, with whose remarkable agility the gentle reader is already familiar, promptly hurled himself after him and pursued him across the garden.

Herr Dapsul von Zabelthau had been watching this dreadful duel, speechless and paralysed with horror, but now he burst out in a cry of anguish:

"Oh, my daughter Anna! Oh, my poor unhappy daughter Anna! Lost… I… you… both of us are lost, lost!"

And with that he dashed out of the room and up the stairs of his astronomical tower as fast as he could go.

Fräulein Ann simply could not think, simply could not imagine what on earth had suddenly plunged her father into such a state of gloom. As far as she was concerned, the whole thing had been extremely enjoyable, and she was still congratulating herself on the discovery that her fiancé possessed not only wealth and rank, but courage into the bargain, for you will not find many girls in this world who are prepared to love a coward. Indeed, now that she had had a demonstration of Daucus Carota's courage, it suddenly struck her how very annoying it was that Herr Amandus von Nebelstern had refused to fight him.

If she had still had any doubts about sacrificing Herr Amandus to King Daucus the First, she would have made up her mind to do so when the full glory of her new engagement was thus revealed to her. She immediately sat down and wrote the following letter:

MY DEAR AMANDUS,

Everything in this world is liable to change and decay, the schoolmaster tells me, and he's absolutely right. I know you're far too wise and learned to disagree with the schoolmaster, my dear Amandus, or to be in the least surprised when I tell you that there's been a slight change in my feelings too. Mind you, I'm still very fond of you, and I can just imagine how handsome you must look in your red velvet cap with the gold tassel, but as for marrying you – well, you see, dear Amandus, although you're so clever and know how to write such beautiful poems, you aren't a king and never will be, and – don't be frightened – but little Herr Corduanspitz isn't Herr Corduanspitz at all, but a powerful king called Daucus Carota the First, who governs the whole great vegetable kingdom and has chosen me to be his queen! And ever since my darling little king abandoned his incognito, he's become ever so much handsomer, and I see now that Papa was quite right when he said the head is man's chief glory, so it can't possibly be too big. What's more, Daucus Carota the First (you see how good I am at remembering his wonderful name and spelling it properly? I'm getting quite used to it now) – well, what I was saying was that my little royal fiancé

CHAPTER 4

has got such absolutely charming manners I simply can't describe them. And what bravery, what courage the man has! Before my very eyes he's just put to flight the Duke of Radishes, who's evidently a vulgar upstart – and wow!... the way he jumped through that window after him, you should have just seen it! Also, I don't suppose my Daucus Carota will think very much of your weapons: he seems quite tough, and I doubt if poems would have any effect on him, however pointed they were. So be a good boy and resign yourself to your fate, dear Amandus, and don't hold it against me that I'm going to be a queen instead of your wife. Cheer up, I'll always be your most affectionate friend – and if at any time you want to enlist in the carrot guards, or perhaps as you're more interested in learning than fighting, at Parsnip University or in the Ministry of Pumpkins, just say the word and your fortune's made. Goodbye, and don't be cross with

Your former fiancée but now well-wishing friend and future queen,

ANNA VON ZABELTHAU

(but soon going to drop the von Zabelthau and be just plain Anna).

PS: I'll also see that you're kept supplied with the finest Virginia tobacco – you can be sure of that. As far as I can make out, smoking won't be allowed at my court, but that's all the more reason why I must have a few beds planted with Virginia tobacco, not too far from the throne, so that I can keep an eye on them myself. Culture and morality demand that I should do so, and my Dauckey will have to make a special law about it.

5

*A frightful catastrophe, and the
course of events thereafter.*

Fräulein Ann had just sent off this letter to Herr Amandus von Nebelstern, when Herr Dapsul von Zabelthau came in.

"Oh, my daughter Anna!" he cried in anguished tones. "How shamefully we have both been deceived! The scoundrel who has got you into his clutches, who gave me to understand that he was Baron Porphyrio von Ockerodastes, otherwise known as Corduanspitz, a scion of the illustrious stock which the glorious gnome Tsilmenech created by his union with the noble abbess of Cordova, this utter scoundrel – learn the truth and sink swooning to the ground – is indeed a gnome, but a gnome of the very lowest order, the one which superintends the growth of vegetables! Tsilmenech, on the contrary, belonged to the very highest class of gnomes, those who are entrusted with the care of diamonds. Then come the gnomes who are responsible for metals, under the personal supervision of His Metallic Majesty, then come the flower gnomes, who are not so grand as the others, for the simple reason that they are dependent on the sylphs... but the vilest and most ignoble of them all are the vegetable gnomes – and as if it weren't bad enough that Corduanspitz is one of them, he is actually their king, and his real name is Daucus Carota!"

Fräulein Ann did not sink swooning to the ground, nor did she show the faintest sign of alarm. She merely smiled – the gentle reader already knows why. Herr Dapsul von Zabelthau, however, was most surprised at this reaction, and started urging her, for Heaven's sake, to realize what a frightful situation she was in, and be properly upset about it. Under the circumstances, she saw no reason to keep the secret any longer, so she explained to her father how the so-called Baron von Corduanspitz had long ago disclosed his real identity, and how ever since then she had found him so lovable that she was quite determined not to marry anyone else. She went on to describe the wonders of the vegetable kingdom into which King Daucus Carota the First had taken her, not forgetting to mention the extraordinary charm of its various inhabitants.

Herr Dapsul von Zabelthau kept beating his hands together and bewailing the wicked cunning shown by the gnome king in adopting such an ingenious and such an audacious method of luring poor Ann into his dark satanic realm.

For, however delightful, Herr Dapsul explained, however delightful and however beneficial an alliance between an elemental spirit and a mortal might be, however good an example of such an alliance might be seen in the marriage between the gnome Tsilmenech and Magdalena de la Cruz

CHAPTER 5

– which was, of course, the reason why the treacherous Daucus Carota claimed to be a scion of that particular stock – the situation was entirely different when it came to the kings and princes of these spiritual communities. And whereas salamander kings were merely bad-tempered, sylph kings merely conceited and watersprite kings merely amorous and inclined to be jealous, gnome kings were notoriously spiteful, vicious and cruel. Moreover, by way of reprisals for the abduction of their subjects by the human race, they were always trying to get control of individual human beings, who then lost all semblance of humanity, became as ugly as the gnomes themselves and descended into the earth, never to be seen again.

Fräulein Ann, however, was evidently unwilling to believe that her darling Daucus was as bad as Herr Dapsul made out, for she merely went on talking about the wonders of the vegetable kingdom, over which she soon hoped to reign.

"Deluded child!" cried Herr Dapsul von Zabelthau in a rage. "Deluded, silly child! Don't you credit your father with enough cabbalistic knowledge to realize that everything that Daucus Carota conjured up before you was merely an illusion? You still don't believe me? Very well. In order to save you, my one and only child, I must convince you that I'm speaking the truth, and conviction must come by very desperate means. Follow me!"

For the second time Fräulein Ann had to enter the observatory. From a large box Herr Dapsul von Zabelthau produced a lot of yellow, red, white and green ribbons, with which he proceeded, after some curious formalities, to encircle Ann from head to foot. He then did the same thing to himself, after which they both very cautiously approached the silken palace of King Daucus Carota the First. Fräulein Ann was now instructed by her papa to unpick one of the seams with a small pair of scissors that they had brought with them, and apply her eye to the opening.

Great heavens! What did she see? Instead of that beautiful kitchen garden, instead of the carrot guards, the dames commanders of the cabbage empire, the lavender pageboys, the lettuce princes and all the wonderful, glorious things that she had seen before, she found herself looking down at a swamp of loathsome, colourless slime. And in this slime all sorts of hideous creatures from the bowels of the earth could be seen moving about. Thick earthworms wriggled slowly round and round, while things like beetles crawled laboriously along on little stumpy legs. On their backs they carried great onions with horrible human faces, who grinned and leered at one another with dull yellow eyes, and tried to seize one another's long hooked noses in their tiny claws, which grew immediately behind their ears, and drag one another down into the slime, while disgusting-looking slugs rolled lazily about, waving their long horns high in the air.

It was such an awful sight that Fräulein Ann nearly fainted with horror. She held both hands in front of her face and ran away as fast as she could.

CHAPTER 5

"Now perhaps you realize," said Herr Dapsul von Zabelthau, "now perhaps you realize how shamefully that odious Daucus Carota deceived you, when he showed you a glorious spectacle that lasted only a few moments? Oh, doubtless he made his subjects put on their best clothes and dressed his soldiers in uniforms in order to give you an impression of dazzling splendour. But now you've seen your future subjects in their true colours, and once you're married to that vile Daucus Carota, you'll have to live in his underground kingdom and never revisit the surface of the earth! And if... oh, oh! What do I see, unhappy father that I am?"

Herr Dapsul von Zabelthau had suddenly become so distraught that Fräulein Ann could only suppose that some new disaster had overtaken him. She enquired anxiously what he was so upset about, but all he could get out through his tears was:

"Oh... my... daugh... ter... how... aw... ful... you... look!"

Fräulein Ann ran up to her bedroom, looked in the mirror and started back in deadly terror.

She had every reason to do so, for what had happened was this: just as Herr Dapsul von Zabelthau was trying to open his daughter's eyes to the danger of gradually ceasing to look like herself and changing little by little into the very image of a real gnome queen, he noticed the horrible transformation that had already taken place. Ann's head had grown a lot bigger, and her skin was now saffron-yellow, which was quite enough in itself to make her look very nasty.

Now, although Fräulein Ann was not particularly vain, she was enough of a girl to realize that ugliness is the greatest and most terrible misfortune that can happen to any of us here below. And then, she had so often thought how glorious it would be to drive to church on Sundays in the eight-horse carriage, with a king at her side and a queen's crown on her head, all dressed in satin and covered with diamonds and gold rings and bracelets, to astonish all the neighbours, not excepting the schoolmaster's wife – perhaps even to overawe the proud ladies of the manor in the village to whose rural deanery Dapsulheim belonged! How often she had indulged in curious daydreams of this kind, and now… Fräulein Ann burst into tears.

"Anna! My daughter Anna, come up here at once!" shouted Herr Dapsul von Zabelthau through his megaphone.

This time Papa was wearing a sort of miner's outfit.

"It's always darkest before the dawn," he began, speaking quite calmly. "I've just learnt that Daucus Carota will remain in his palace all day, perhaps until midday tomorrow. He's summoned the whole royal family, all his cabinet ministers and various other high officials of the kingdom for a discussion on the future of kale. It will be a very important meeting, and may go on so long that we shan't have any kale at all this winter. While it's in progress, Daucus Carota will be far too busy with affairs of state to notice what I'm doing, and I shall therefore take the opportunity to prepare a secret weapon which may enable me to resist and overcome the wicked gnome, so that he's forced to go away and leave you alone. Now, while I'm working on it, I want you to keep your eye glued to that telescope and report immediately if you see anyone looking out of the pavilion, or even more important, coming out."

Fräulein Ann did as she was told, but the pavilion remained closed. From time to time, however, in spite of the fact that Herr Dapsul was hammering loudly away at some metal plates just behind her, she heard from the direction of the pavilion a confused sound of shouting, followed by a series of sharp slapping noises, as though people were having their ears boxed. She reported as much to Herr Dapsul von Zabelthau, who replied that he was very glad to hear it, for the more they quarrelled among themselves, the less likely they were to notice what was being forged elsewhere for their destruction.

When the hammering was over, Fräulein Ann was surprised to see that Herr Dapsul von Zabelthau had constructed two lovely copper saucepans and some equally delightful stew pans of the same material. Having run an expert eye over them, and satisfied herself that the quality of the tin-plating was well up to the proper standard, she asked if she might take the splendid utensils away for use in the kitchen. But Herr Dapsul only smiled mysteriously and answered:

"All in good time, my daughter Anna, all in good time! For the moment, my dear child, just go downstairs and wait quietly for further developments."

Herr Dapsul von Zabelthau had smiled, that was the great thing, and poor Ann immediately began to feel more hopeful.

Shortly before noon on the following day, Herr Dapsul came down into the kitchen with his saucepans and stew pans and told Fräulein Ann and the maid to go away, as he wished to cook lunch himself. He also gave Fräulein Ann special instructions to be as polite and affectionate as she possibly could towards Corduanspitz, who would doubtless arrive at any moment.

A few minutes later, sure enough, Herr Corduanspitz, or rather King Daucus Carota the First, put in an appearance, and much as he had seemed in love before, he now seemed positively transported with joy at the sight of Fräulein Ann. To her horror, she discovered that she had already become too small for Daucus to have the slightest difficulty in jumping onto her lap and covering her face with kisses – which the poor girl had to put up with, although she felt absolutely revolted by the odious little monster.

Eventually Herr Dapsul von Zabelthau came in and said:

"Ah, my dear Porphyrio von Ockerodastes! Won't you come into the kitchen and see how efficiently your future wife has organized everything there?"

CHAPTER 5

With a crafty, gloating expression on his face, such as Ann had never seen on it before, he seized little Daucus by the arm and practically dragged him out of the room and into the kitchen.

At a sign from her father Fräulein Ann followed, and her spirits rose at the sight of the splendid fire that was blazing and crackling in the grate, and the handsome copper saucepans and stew pans that were simmering on the range.

As Herr Dapsul von Zabelthau led Corduanspitz towards them, all the pots and pans started sizzling and bubbling more and more loudly, until finally the sizzles and bubbles turned into agonized whimpers and groans, and from one of the saucepans came the following desperate entreaty:

"Oh, Daucus Carota! Oh, Your Majesty! Please rescue your loyal subjects! Please rescue us poor carrots! We've been chopped to pieces, thrown into dirty water, smothered in butter and salt, and our sufferings are quite inexpressible – sufferings which we share with some noble young sprigs of parsley!"

Then from a stew pan came the cry:

"Oh, Daucus Carota! Oh, Your Majesty! Please rescue your loyal subjects! Please rescue us poor carrots! We're roasting in hell, and we're so short of water that our dreadful thirst compels us to drink our own heart's blood!"

Then from another saucepan came the piteous plea:

"Oh, Daucus Carota! Oh, Your Majesty! Please rescue your loyal subjects! Please rescue us poor carrots! A cruel cook has gouged out our insides and stuffed us up with all sorts of foreign bodies like eggs and butter and cream, so that all our ideas and intellectual faculties are utterly confused, and we don't even know what we're thinking!"

Finally, from all the saucepans and stew pans rose a simultaneous chorus of shrieks and groans:

"Oh, Daucus Carota! Mighty king! Rescue, please rescue your loyal subjects! Please rescue us poor carrots!"

"What damned silly nonsense is this?" shouted Corduanspitz, and, leaping with his usual agility onto the kitchen range, he inspected the contents of one of the saucepans, then suddenly plunged inside it.

Quick as a flash, Herr Dapsul von Zabelthau sprang to clap down the saucepan lid on top of him, triumphantly crying, "Caught!" But with all the resilience of a rubber ball Herr Corduanspitz came bouncing back out of the saucepan and gave Herr Dapsul von Zabelthau a resounding box on the ear, yelling:

"You stupid, insolent cabbalist, you'll pay for this! Out, lads, out this instant!"

Immediately hundreds and hundreds of nasty little men no bigger than a finger came swarming out of all the pots and pans like a miniature Wild Hunt,* attached themselves to every portion of Herr Dapsul von Zabelthau's anatomy, hurled him over backwards into a big dish and proceeded to season and garnish him by emptying out the stock from the saucepans and stew pans all over him, and sprinkling him with chopped egg, grated nutmeg and breadcrumbs. Daucus Carota then disappeared through the window, and his subjects followed suit.

Fräulein Ann collapsed in horror beside the dish on which her poor papa lay seasoned and garnished. She thought he must be dead, for he did not show the slightest sign of life.

"Oh, poor Papa!" she wailed. "Now you're dead, and there's no one to save me from that fiendish Daucus!"

But at this point Herr Dapsul von Zabelthau opened his eyes, sprang with renewed energy from the dish and shrieked in a ghastly voice that Fräulein Ann had never heard him use before:

"Ha, Daucus Carota, you scoundrel, I'm not at the end of my rope yet! You'll soon see what the stupid, insolent cabbalist can do!"

So Fräulein Ann hurriedly brushed the chopped egg, grated nutmeg and breadcrumbs off him with the kitchen broom, after which he seized a copper saucepan, stuck it on his head like a helmet, grasped a stew pan in his left hand and a great iron kitchen ladle in his right and, thus armed and accoutred, went dashing out of the house. The last Fräulein Ann saw of him, he was running at full speed towards Corduanspitz's pavilion, and yet remaining absolutely stationary. Then she lost consciousness.

When she recovered, Herr Dapsul von Zabelthau had disappeared, and she felt horribly anxious about him when he failed to return that evening, or that night, or the following day. She could only conclude that the second method of attack had been even less successful than the first.

6

*The last and most edifying
chapter in the book.*

Fräulein Ann was sitting all by herself in her room, feeling deeply depressed, when suddenly the door opened, and who should come in but Herr Amandus von Nebelstern! Overcome with shame and remorse, she burst into a flood of tears.

"Oh, my darling Amandus," she sobbed, "do forgive me for all the silly things I said in my letter. I was absolutely bewitched when I wrote it – in fact, I still am. Please, please help me, Amandus darling! I know I'm all nasty and yellow to look at, but my heart's still as faithful as ever, and I don't want to be a queen after all!"

"My dear girl," replied Amandus von Nebelstern, "I really don't know what you're worrying about. You seem to have done extremely well for yourself."

"Oh, please, don't make fun of me," cried Ann. "I've been punished enough already for being so silly and conceited."

"No, quite seriously," continued Herr Amandus von Nebelstern, "I simply don't understand you, my darling girl. To be absolutely frank, I must admit that your last letter put me in a tearing rage. I thrashed my gyp, and then my poodle, and smashed several glasses – for you know we students are liable to get pretty savage when we're roused. But when I'd calmed down a bit, I decided to come over here right away and see for myself how, why and to whom I'd lost my beloved fiancée. Love makes no distinction of class and rank, and I meant to have it out with King Daucus Carota as man to man, and ask him whether I shouldn't be justified in taking it as a personal insult if he went and married my girl. However, when I got here, things turned out rather differently. As I was walking past that very fine pavilion that's been put up over there, King Daucus Carota came out, and I soon discovered that he's quite the most delightful king in the world – though admittedly to date I haven't met any others. For just imagine, my dear girl: he immediately recognized my genius for poetry, said some very kind things about my poems, although he hadn't even read them, and offered me the post of Poet Laureate! Well, of course it's the sort of job that I've always longed for, so I was only too glad to accept. Oh, my precious creature, what inspired odes I shall write about you! You see, it's perfectly all right for a poet to be in love with a queen or a princess – in fact, it's really part of his duties to lose his heart to some royal personage or other. And if he goes mad as a result, well, it's a short cut to that divine frenzy without which no poetry can be written. So you must never be surprised if a poet behaves rather oddly. Think of the great poet, Tasso, who's said to have suffered from a certain lack of common sense as a result of falling in love with the Princess Leonora d'Este.* In short, my darling, even though you'll soon be a queen, you'll always remain the mistress of my heart, and I'll raise your name to the stars in verses of the most divine sublimity!"

"What! Do you mean to say you've actually seen the beastly little creature, and he's—" burst out Fräulein Ann in amazement, but at that moment in walked the little gnome king himself, and addressed her tenderly as follows:

"Ah, my dear, sweet, adorable fiancée! Don't be frightened, I'm not at all cross about that little breach of taste committed by Herr Dapsul von Zabelthau. Quite the contrary, for it's been the unexpected means of bringing my happiness even nearer. Yes, dearest, the wedding will take place tomorrow. You'll also be glad to hear that I've appointed Herr Amandus von Nebelstern our Poet Laureate, and I want him to give us a specimen of his talents right away. But first we'll go into the summer house, for I prefer to be out of doors. I'll sit on your lap, my love, and while he's singing to us, you can scratch my head for me. It's a thing I'm very fond of on these occasions."

Fräulein Ann was too paralysed with terror to raise any objection. So out they went into the summer house, where Daucus Carota sat on her lap and had his head scratched, while Herr Amandus von Nebelstern began, to his own accompaniment on the guitar, the first of twelve dozen songs, written and composed by himself, all collected in a very fat volume.

Unfortunately the *Chronicle of Dapsulheim*, on which this story is based, does not contain the full text of the songs in question. It merely states that passing peasants stopped and wondered who on earth it could be that was going through such agonies in Herr Dapsul von Zabelthau's summer house, and uttering such horrible cries of pain.

Daucus Carota started writhing about on Fräulein Ann's lap, and moaning and groaning more and more pathetically, as if he had got a frightful stomach ache. She also noticed, to her great surprise, that as the recital proceeded he seemed to be getting rapidly smaller and smaller.

Finally, Herr Amandus von Nebelstern sang the following sublime verses (the only ones that are actually recorded in the *Chronicle*):

> Oh, how blithe the poet's song!
> Scents of flowers and bright dreams
> Draw his trancèd soul along
> Through a heaven of rosy gleams
> To a glorious golden sphere
> Floating upon waves of flowers,
> Where enchanted rainbows rear
> Arches o'er celestial bowers.
> When the heart is light and gay,
> It can only trust and love,

CHAPTER 6

> So the poet in his lay
> Bills and coos like any dove.
> Then he spreads his wings and flies
> To some far mysterious jail,
> While from out his lustrous eyes
> Glimmers his eternal soul.
> And should e'er his inmost part
> Feel the promptings of desire,
> Instantly his mighty heart
> Bursts into a blaze of fire,
> And with kisses and caresses,
> Goaded by delirious passion,
> Yearning for togethernesses
> Far beyond our human fashion,
> Drawn by flower scents and dreams,
> Seeds of life, of love, of hope,
> And by—

At this point Daucus Carota gave a loud shriek and turned into a tiny little carrot, which slipped off Ann's lap, plunged into the ground and disappeared. Simultaneously the grey toadstool which had apparently grown during the night, quite close to where she was sitting on the grass, shot up into the air. But it was not a toadstool after all: it was the grey felt hat of Herr Dapsul von Zabelthau, and there he was in person underneath it! He flung his arms round Herr Amandus von Nebelstern's neck and exclaimed delightedly:

"Oh, my dear sir! My beloved friend! My most excellent Herr Amandus von Nebelstern! Your powerful incantations have brought crashing to the ground all my pretensions to cabbalistic wisdom! Where the philosopher's strongest magic and most desperate courage had failed, your poems were successful, acting upon the treacherous Daucus Carota like some deadly poison, so that in spite of his gnomish nature he would have died miserably of colic, had he not quickly taken refuge in his own kingdom! You have liberated my daughter Anna and released me from the dreadful spell that kept me rooted here, to all appearances a common toadstool, liable to be slaughtered at any moment by the hands of my own daughter – for the dear girl is quite merciless to every form of fungus, and puts them all to the edge of the spade, unless they can, like mushrooms, produce immediate evidence of good character. You have earned my most heartfelt, most fervent gratitude, and... am I right in supposing, my dear Herr Amandus von Nebelstern, that your feelings towards my daughter remain unchanged? She has, I fear, lost some of her physical charms through the villainy of that malignant gnome, but no doubt you are far too good a philosopher to—"

"Oh, Papa! Dearest Papa!" came a joyful cry from Fräulein Ann. "Oh, look! Do look! The silk palace has disappeared! That ugly little monster's gone away altogether, complete with all his lettuce princes and pumpkin cabinet ministers and goodness knows what else!"

CHAPTER 6

With these words Fräulein Ann went dashing off towards the kitchen garden. Herr Dapsul von Zabelthau ran after her, as fast as he could go, and Herr Amandus von Nebelstern followed, grumbling to himself:

"Well, I really don't know what to think of it all, but one thing's clear enough anyway: that nasty little carrot chap's an absolute fraud! He can't have any real feeling for poetry, or he wouldn't have got stomach ache in the middle of my best songs, and slunk away into the ground like that!"

As she entered the kitchen garden, where there was not a single green leaf to be seen, Fräulein Ann felt a dreadful pain in the finger with the ring on it. At the same moment, a heart-rending cry was heard from underground, and the tip of a carrot poked up through the soil. Instinctively, Fräulein Ann knew what to do: she slipped the ring quite easily off her finger, a thing she had never been able to do before, and popped it onto the carrot, which promptly disappeared, and the heart-rending cry died away into silence. The same instant, wonderful to relate, Fräulein Ann became as pretty as before, as well proportioned and as white as anyone could reasonably expect a hard-working country girl to be. Fräulein Ann and Herr Dapsul von Zabelthau let out a simultaneous cry of joy, while Herr Amandus von Nebelstern stood gaping open-mouthed, and still did not know what to think of it all.

The housemaid now came running up with a spade. Fräulein Ann took it from her, and, crying "Now let's get to work!", brandished it triumphantly in the air. Unfortunately, in doing so, she hit Herr Amandus von Nebelstern very hard on the head, precisely at the point where the seat of consciousness is said to be located, with the result that he dropped like a dead man to the ground.

Flinging the murderous implement away, Fräulein Ann threw herself down beside her loved one and burst into desperate cries of grief, while the housemaid poured the entire contents of a watering can all over him, and Herr Dapsul von Zabelthau went dashing off to his observatory, to find out from the stars if Herr Amandus von Nebelstern was really dead or not.

Before long, however, Herr Amandus opened his eyes, jumped up and, dripping wet as he was, folded Fräulein Ann in his arms, exclaiming in accents of passionate love:

"Oh, my dearest, darling Ann! We're together again at last!"

This accident had a remarkable, in fact an almost incredible effect on the young lovers, which soon manifested itself in a curious transformation of their mental attitudes.

Fräulein Ann developed a horror of handling a spade, and from then on governed the vegetable kingdom like a real queen, watching over the interests of her subjects with loving care and seeing that they were properly looked after, but never doing a hand's turn herself, and leaving all that sort of thing to her faithful retainers.

Herr Amandus von Nebelstern came to the conclusion that everything he had written and all his poetical aspirations were supremely silly, and devoted himself to the study of the really great poets of ancient and modern times, thus filling his mind so completely with their inspiring productions that there was no room left for any thoughts about his own self. He came to believe that a poem must be something more than a mass of confused verbiage churned out in a state of vacuous delirium – and, having burnt all the attempts at poetry on which he had prided himself, half jokingly and half seriously, in the past, he became a more sensible and generally brighter lad than he had been before.

One morning, Herr Dapsul von Zabelthau really did come down from his astronomical tower and take Fräulein Ann and Herr Amandus von Nebelstern to church for their wedding.

And they lived very happily ever after, but whether anything ever came of the projected union between Herr Dapsul von Zabelthau and the sylph Nehalilah, the *Chronicle of Dapsulheim* makes no mention.

Notes

p. 15, *M. le Baron de Thunder-ten-Tronck*: A character from Voltaire's *Candide*.

p. 32, *the Green Vault at Dresden*: The Grünes Gewölbe, a museum in Dresden founded in 1723.

p. 37, *Count of Mirandola*: The Italian natural philosopher Giovanni Pico della Mirandola (1463–94), renowned for his interest in esoteric sciences and magic.

p. 40, *Magdalena de la Cruz*: A Franciscan nun of Córdoba (1487–1560). She was honoured for many years as a living saint, but her stigmata were later exposed to be fraudulent, and the Inquisition condemned her to perpetual imprisonment.

p. 45, *Lactantius or St Thomas Aquinas*: Lactantius (*c*.250–*c*.325) was an early Christian apologist and Church Father; St Thomas Aquinas (*c*.1225–1274) was a famous Christian theologian.

p. 46, *Apollo Belvedere... Dying Gladiator*: The *Apollo Belvedere* is a celebrated sculpture from classical times. The *Dying Gladiator* (also known as the *Dying Gaul*) is a famous Roman copy of a now lost Greek sculpture from the Hellenistic period.

p. 50, *turned into a pillar of salt, like Lot's wife*: See Genesis 19:26.

p. 51, *Pan Kapustowicz... Rocambole of France*: The names are all suggestive, in their respective languages, of edible garden plants.

p. 54, *cordovan or morocco*: Cordovan and morocco are two kinds of fine leather made from goatskin.

p. 59, *Lord Chesterfield... Knigge... Madame de Genlis*: Philip Stanhope, 4th Earl of Chesterfield (1694–1773), is now mostly remembered for his educative *Letters to his Son* (1774); the German writer Adolph Freiherr Knigge (1752–96) was the author of *On Human Relations* (1788), covering the fields of good behaviour, politeness and etiquette; Caroline-Stéphanie-Félicité du Crest de Saint-Aubin (1746–1830), also known as Madame de Genlis, was a French author and educator.

p. 68, *Tyrtaean war songs*: Tyrtaeus (fl. mid-7th century BC) was a poet from Sparta, a famously warlike nation. Only fragments of his poetry have survived.

p. 70, *Tieck... Friedrich Richter*: The German writer and critic Ludwig Tieck (1773–1853) and the German novelist Johann Paul Friedrich Richter, better known as Jean Paul (1763–1825).

p. 72, *la beauté du diable de la jeunesse*: "The beauty of the devil of youth" (French).

p. 86, *Wild Hunt*: A European folk myth about a spectral group of horsemen.

NOTES

p. 91, *Tasso… Princess Leonora d'Este*: The Italian poet Torquato Tasso (1544–95) was confined for mental-health problems, which were said to have been worsened by his love for Princess Leonora, sister of Duke Alfonso II (1533–97), under whom he served.

EVERGREENS SERIES
Beautifully produced classics, affordably priced

Alma Classics is committed to making available a wide range of literature from around the globe. Most of the titles are enriched by an extensive critical apparatus, notes and extra reading material, as well as a selection of photographs. The texts are based on the most authoritative editions and edited using a fresh, accessible editorial approach. With an emphasis on production, editorial and typographical values, Alma Classics aspires to revitalize the whole experience of reading classics.

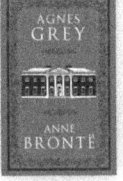

On the Origin of Species
Charles Darwin
Daniel Defoe
Moll Flanders
Charles Dickens
A Christmas Carol
David Copperfield
Charles Dickens
Great Expectations
Charles Dickens
Hard Times
Charles Dickens
Charles Dickens
Oliver Twist
Charles Dickens
A Tale of Two Cities
The Double
Fyodor Dostoevsky
Fyodor Dostoevsky
The Gambler
The Idiot
Fyodor Dostoevsky
Notes from Underground
Fyodor Dostoevsky
Middlemarch
George Eliot
The Mill on the Floss
George Eliot
Praise of Folly
Erasmus
The Beautiful and Damned
F. Scott Fitzgerald
The Great Gatsby
F. Scott Fitzgerald
Tender is the Night
F. Scott Fitzgerald
Gustave Flaubert
Madame Bovary
North and South
Elizabeth Gaskell
The Sorrows of Young Werther
Goethe
Dead Souls
Nikolai Gogol
Nikolai Gogol
Petersburg Tales
Thomas Hardy
Far from the Madding Crowd
Thomas Hardy
Jude the Obscure
Thomas Hardy
Tess of the D'Urbervilles
Nathaniel Hawthorne
The Scarlet Letter
The Portrait of a Lady
Henry James
Three Men in a Boat
Jerome K. Jerome
Dubliners
James Joyce
Ulysses
James Joyce
Franz Kafka
Metamorphosis
Franz Kafka
The Trial
Lady Chatterley's Lover
D.H. Lawrence
Sons and Lovers
D.H. Lawrence
Mikhail Lermontov
A Hero of Our Time

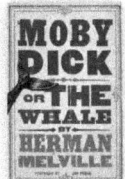

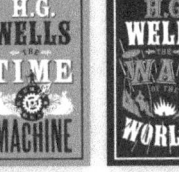

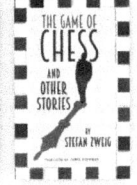

For our complete list and latest offers

visit

almabooks.com/evergreens

101-PAGE CLASSICS
Great Rediscovered Classics

This series has been created with the aim to redefine and enrich the classics canon by promoting unjustly neglected works of enduring significance. These works, beautifully produced and mostly in translation, will intrigue and inspire the literary connoisseur and the general reader alike.

THE PERFECT COLLECTION OF LESSER-KNOWN WORKS BY MAJOR AUTHORS

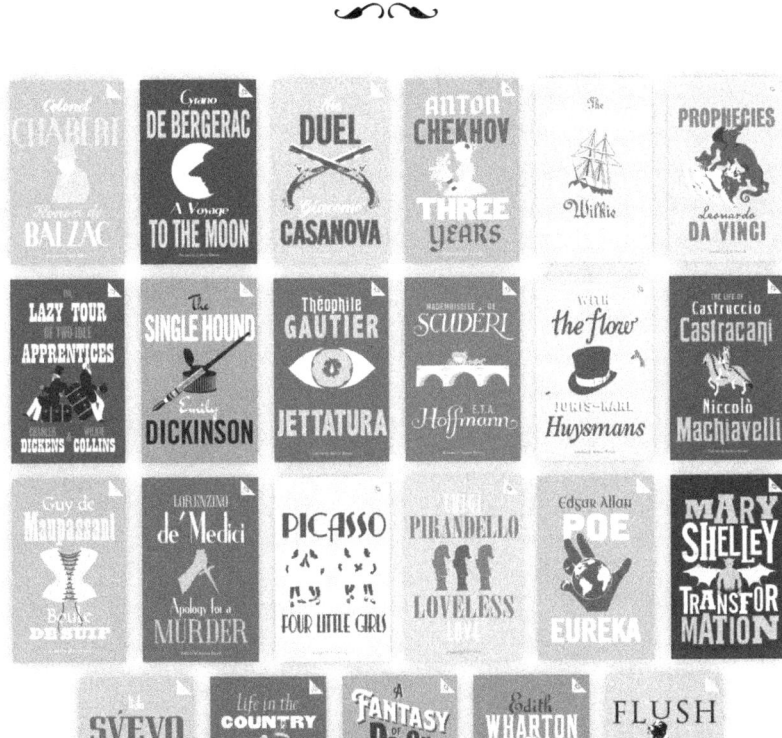

almabooks.com/101-pages

GREAT POETS SERIES

Each volume is based on the most authoritative text, and reflects Alma's commitment to provide affordable editions with valuable insight into the great poets' works.

Selected Poems
Blake, William
ISBN: 9781847498212
£7.99 • PB • 288 pp

The Rime of the Ancient Mariner
Coleridge, Samuel Taylor
ISBN: 9781847497529
£7.99 • PB • 256 pp

Complete Poems
Keats, John
ISBN: 9781847497567
£9.99 • PB • 520 pp

Paradise Lost
Milton, John
ISBN: 9781847498038
£7.99 • PB • 320 pp

Sonnets
Shakespeare, William
ISBN: 9781847496089
£4.99 • PB • 256 pp

Leaves of Grass
Whitman, Walt
ISBN: 9781847497550
£8.99 • PB • 288 pp

MORE POETRY TITLES

Dante Alighieri: *Inferno, Purgatory, Paradise, Rime, Vita Nuova, Love Poems*; Alexander Pushkin: *Lyrics Vol. 1 and 2, Love Poems, Ruslan and Lyudmila*; François Villon: *The Testament and Other Poems*; Cecco Angiolieri: *Sonnets*; Guido Cavalcanti: *Complete Poems*; Emily Brontë: *Poems from the Moor*; Anonymous: *Beowulf*; Ugo Foscolo: *Sepulchres*; W.B. Yeats: *Selected Poems*; Charles Baudelaire: *The Flowers of Evil*; Sándor Márai: *The Withering World*; Antonia Pozzi: *Poems*; Giuseppe Gioacchino Belli: *Sonnets*; Dickens: *Poems*

WWW.ALMABOOKS.COM/POETRY

ALMA CLASSICS

ALMA CLASSICS aims to publish mainstream and lesser-known European classics in an innovative and striking way, while employing the highest editorial and production standards. By way of a unique approach the range offers much more, both visually and textually, than readers have come to expect from contemporary classics publishing.

LATEST TITLES PUBLISHED BY ALMA CLASSICS

473. Sinclair Lewis, *Babbitt*
474. Edith Wharton, *The House of Mirth*
475. George Orwell, *Burmese Days*
476. Virginia Woolf, *The Voyage Out*
477. Charles Dickens, *Pictures from Italy*
478. Fyodor Dostoevsky, *Crime and Punishment*
479. Anton Chekhov, *Small Fry and Other Stories*
480. George Orwell, *Homage to Catalonia*
481. Carlo Collodi, *The Adventures of Pinocchio*
482. Virginia Woolf, *Between the Acts*
483. Alain Robbe-Grillet, *Last Year at Marienbad*
484. Charles Dickens, *The Pickwick Papers*
485. Wilkie Collins, *The Haunted Hotel*
486. Ivan Turgenev, *Parasha and Other Poems*
487. Arthur Conan Doyle, *His Last Bow*
488. Ivan Goncharov, *The Frigate Pallada*
489. Arthur Conan Doyle, *The Casebook of Sherlock Holmes*
490. Alexander Pushkin, *Lyrics Vol. 4*
491. Arthur Conan Doyle, *The Valley of Fear*
492. Gottfried Keller, *Green Henry*
493. Grimmelshausen, *Simplicius Simplicissimus*
494. Edgar Allan Poe, *The Raven and Other Poems*
495. Sinclair Lewis, *Main Street*
496. Prosper Mérimée, *Carmen*
497. D.H. Lawrence, *Women in Love*
498. Albert Maltz, *A Tale of One January*
499. George Orwell, *Coming Up for Air*
500. Anton Chekhov, *The Looking Glass and Other Stories*
501. Ivan Goncharov, *An Uncommon Story*
502. Paul Éluard, *Selected Poems*
503. Ivan Turgenev, *Memoirs of a Hunter*
504. Albert Maltz, *A Long Day in a Short Life*
505. Edith Wharton, *Ethan Frome*
506. Charles Dickens, *The Old Curiosity Shop*
507. Fyodor Dostoevsky, *The Village of Stepanchikovo*
508. George Orwell, *The Clergyman's Daughter*
509. Virginia Woolf, *The New Dress and Other Stories*
510. Ivan Goncharov, *A Serendipitous Error and Two Incidents at Sea*
511. Beatrix Potter, *Peter Rabbit*

www.almaclassics.com